PARAMOUNT PICTURES PRESENTS

A NICITA/LLOYD PRODUCTION A JOHN BADHAM MOVIE

WESLEY SNIPES

DROP ZONE

GARY BUSEY YANCY BUTLER MICHAEL JETER

MUSIC BY HANS ZIMMER EDITED BY FRANK MORRISS

PRODUCTION DESIGNER JOE ALVES DIRECTOR OF PHOTOGRAPHY ROY H. WAGNER, A.S.C.

CO-PRODUCER DOUG CLAYBOURNE EXECUTIVE PRODUCER JOHN BADHAM

STORY BY TONY GRIFFIN & GUY MANOS & PETER BARSOCCHINI

SCREENPLAY BY PETER BARSOCCHINI and JOHN BISHOP

PRODUCED BY D.J. CARUSO, WALLIS NICITA and LAUREN LLOYD

DIRECTED BY JOHN BADHAM

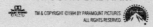

DROP ZONE

A Novel by Robert Tine. Based upon DROP ZONE
Story by Tony Griffin & Guy Manos & Peter Barsocchini
Screenplay by Peter Barsocchini and John Bishop

JOVE BOOKS, NEW YORK

DROP ZONE

A Jove Book / published by arrangement with
Paramount Licensing Group

PRINTING HISTORY
Jove edition / January 1995

ISBN: 0-515-11645-9

A JOVE BOOK®
Jove Books are published by The Berkley Publishing Group,
200 Madison Avenue, New York, New York 10016.
JOVE and the "J" design are trademarks
belonging to Jove Publications, Inc.

PRINTED IN THE UNITED STATES OF AMERICA

10   9   8   7   6   5   4   3

1

There are no good prisons, but some are worse—much worse—than others.

As bad prisons go, the Southland Federal Penitentiary was close to the bottom of the scale, a remote, grim lock-up for unregenerate hard cases—the prison system called them recidivists—situated on a small patch of dry land in the middle of ten thousand acres of hot, smelly swamp in southernmost South Florida. Earl Leedy called it home and he liked it; he felt safe there.

Of course, Earl Leedy was not your common or garden variety penal institution thug. For one thing, out of step with his fellow inmates whom he considered Neanderthal dim-bulb goons with no more intelligence than you could fit in a walnut, Earl Leedy was a genius; a bona-fide, MENSA-certified, stratospheric IQ genius, with a head for figures and logical thinking that outstripped all but the most powerful main-frame computers. Of course, it goes without saying, given that he was in prison, Earl Leedy was an *evil* genius.

But then, Leedy differed from the other inmates at Southland in so many ways. Virtually all of the prisoners were incarcerated for crimes of violence—everything from rape to armed robbery to murder in the first degree—yet Earl Leedy hated physical violence with a passion.

Other prisoners swaggered around the yard and the cell blocks daring anyone to challenge them—it was their way of making themselves big men. But, unfortunately for some, from time to time the challenge was taken up and a big man ended up dead or worse, from the perspective of the joint, humiliated.

Earl Leedy hated confrontation of any kind; he got violently ill at the sight of blood, could not even stand to *think* of pain without the very real danger of keeling over in a dead faint.

But the biggest difference between Earl and the rest of the prisoners in Southland, was that Earl Leedy was a snitch and, as such, was decidedly unpopular with the other inmates. Of course, Earl didn't consider himself a rat and he wasn't, in the sense that he was spying on the other prisoners or telling the authorities about hidden weapons, secret liquor stills, or intramural gang vendettas.

No. Earl Leedy considered himself a highly placed informant assisting the United States government in the investigation of a major drug smuggling and money laundering operation. He thought of himself as an undercover agent, a secret operative moving like a shark through the dangerous waters of international crime syndicates. In actual fact, he had been a money man and computer whiz for a drug cartel and had cut a deal to save his own skin. The government had parked him in Southland to keep him safe until he was called upon to testify in a whole series of high profile federal cases in trials to be convened all over the country.

So, until the Feds put the finishing touches on their legal actions, Earl Leedy had little to do beside stay in his cell, read, think, and take care of the cats he had discovered in his small corner of the prison exercise yard.

The prisoners in the row of cells on Leedy's tier were allotted ninety minutes of exercise time every day, an hour and a half that most of the men devoted to strenuous exercise. They worked out with weights, sparred and shadow boxed, or played an endless game of basketball on the steaming hot asphalt, under the white disc of the South Florida sun.

Each part of the yard was carefully segregated along racial lines, divisions laid down not by the prison authorities but by the prisoners themselves. The separation of races was so absolute that a newcomer to the yard, blindfolded, would have been able to tell one segment from another.

Each race possessed a big boom box, a brace of powerful speakers dueling in the confined space of the yard. The black prisoners exercised and played basketball to the angry, insistent, thumping accompaniment of rap. The whites favored the noisy, frantic thrash of acid rock or, when the southern contingent was on the asphalt, the plaintive, saccharine whine of country music. Hispanics were always in a constant wrangle over which kind of brassy salsa they would listen to, depending on country of origin—Cuba, Puerto Rico, Mexico, Colombia.

Earl Leedy was kept seperate from the rest of the prisoners and that suited him just fine. When the buzzer sounded on his tier, marking the commencement of the exercise period, all of the cells doors slid open, controlled by remote from the tier guard's armored blockhouse. All of them opened, that is, except Earl Leedy's. Once the prisoners had been escorted from the level, his cell door opened and Earl Leedy was allowed out to take his exercise alone.

Before he had gotten in trouble with the law, Leedy had read about prisoners suing the Department of Corrections and the Federal Government, claiming that their rights were violated when prison authorities chose not to put them in with the rest of the jail population. Leedy couldn't understand why someone would get upset about an arrangement like that. Based on what he had seen of the general population of this or any other prison, Leedy was damn glad he was kept apart—the solitude of his life behind bars didn't bother him a bit, particularly when one considered the alternative. Even if people didn't want to kill him because of what he was, he doubted that he would have been able to withstand the constant noise, dirt and crudity of daily life in a prison—never mind rape, mutilation, murder and assault. Leedy was quite happy where he was, as long as he had something to read—and, of course, his precious kitty cats to take care of.

As he passed through the lockup, a guard slipped Leedy a parcel wrapped in newspaper and Earl paused to look inside. He fixed a baleful stare on the guard, the corners of his mouth turned down in disappointment.

"Looks like a lot of fat," he said.

"What's the matter, Leedy? Your goddamn pussies got high cholesterol?"

"No," said Leedy primly. "And I don't want them to acquire that condition, either."

The day was a hot one and the corrections officer was tired—he had been on duty since five that morning—and most of all, he hated special treatment for prisoners. It made his already difficult job that much harder to perform. He slapped his billy club on the steel railing of the tier. "Just move it, would 'ya?"

"*Alone*?" asked Leedy.

4

"Come on," grumbled the guard. "Let's get a move on. I'm right behind you."

The guard escorted Leedy down two flights of metal stairs and out onto the exercise yard. They crossed the half acre of open space, ignored by all the prisoners— Leedy's little stroll across the yard was routine and unremarkable—ignored by all the prisoners except one, that is. The lone exception, a huge white con with dark tattoos on every square inch of his powerfully muscled arms watched Leedy intently, following him with his eyes to the far end of the enclosure where Leedy stopped and waited for the guard to unlock a gate. This lead to an alley where it was thought that Leedy could exercise in relative safety.

"I'll be back," said the guard.

Leedy walked to the corner of the building to the point where a drainage pipe emerged from the wall. He glanced cautiously to the right and left, before getting down on his knees and unwrapping the small package of food.

"Here kitty, kitty, kitty—" he cooed into the pipe. "Come on girls . . ."

Almost immediately, a fat white cat popped out of the dark hole followed by a smaller, younger Abyssinian. The cats mewed loudly and rubbed against him, glad to see him. Leedy's eyes sparkled. He was glad to see his feline friends too—they were the only living creatures in the whole prison, probably the whole state, who actually liked him.

Earl scooped the white cat up in his arms and scratched the soft fur on her throat. "How have you been, Agnes? I was worried about you . . ." Leedy adopted that phony sweet voice that people use when talking to small animals and babies.

The cat purred deeply. The ginger cat meowed despon-

5

dently, downcast at having been cut out of the affection of the master. Leedy laughed and picked him up too.

"Sorry, Cleo, I didn't mean to ignore you. My mistake . . . my mistake . . ." Carefully he put the animals down on the cracked concrete. "Let's see what we have for your lunch . . ." He peered at the scraps, leftovers from the breakfast served that morning in the prison cafeteria. "We have some bacon," he said, "and some eggs . . . and some . . . I don't know what that is . . ." He poked at some grayish brown matter that could have been bread or oatmeal. Daintily, he picked it out of the mush and threw it away. "Don't eat that. Bad. Ech." The two cats pushed their faces into the oily leftovers, tearing into the food voraciously.

"There you go, honey-pies," said Leedy, happy to see them eat so heartily. He had his back to the yard, completely oblivious to the activity there.

He did not see the big convict walk over to one of the big boom boxes and pull the antenna off the back, then amble casually toward the gate leading to Leedy's private little corner. Keeping his hands at his sides and his body blocking any view from the guard tower, the con slid open the antenna, locking it open at its fullest extension. The thin shaft of steel had been sharpened to a deadly point. No one noticed him slip through the gate.

Least of all Leedy. He was still bent over his furry little friends, watching them eat, completely oblivious to the danger bearing down on him.

"Agnes pretty baby," he said, his voice all soft and sugary, "eat your lunch, now honeykins . . ."

As if his cloying words were putting the cat off her food, she looked up and opened her mouth wide, flexing her jaws. Then, without warning, Agnes arched her back and hissed, jumping straight into the air. Leedy saw a

6

shadow fall across him and knew instantly what was coming.

"Oh my God!" Leedy threw his wiry frame to one side, feeling the wind of the homemade knife passing just inches from the skin on his neck.

"Fuck," grunted the con.

"Help!" Leedy screeched.

He tumbled headlong into the mess of greasy newspaper and bacon rinds, the cats scattered as the food went flying.

"Hold still," the convict said as he lashed out again, as if annoyed that his victim would not cooperate in his own murder. Earl Leedy couldn't help but notice that the big man had a very determined look on his face, as if killing him was the most important thing on his mind. Leedy scrambled away like a crab, whimpering in terror.

He filled his lungs with air and screamed like a man possessed. "Somebody! Help me! Please!"

In the yard, the volume on all three boom boxes—black, white and Hispanic—got bumped up a notch.

A grimy hand reached out and grabbed Leedy by the throat. "Shuttup." He smacked Leedy in the face as if he was nothing more than a recalcitrant child unreasonably demanding something not good for him. Then he clapped his thick, calloused hand across Leedy's mouth, immediately cutting off Earl's frantic screams.

The big convict reared back with his other hand, the pointed weapon glittering for a moment in the sunlight. Earl's eyes grew wide, sure that this was the end. He gave one last frantic squirm, but the man's strong arms held him tight.

Then—crack!—a shiny black billy club smacked hard into the side of the con's head, the force of the blow pitching him forward. He was out cold before he hit the ground, slamming face first onto the hot concrete, his eyes wide and staring, blood trickling from his mouth.

Leedy broke free, his chest heaving as he gasped for air, staring up into the face of the prison guard. The CO was standing over the con, his club ready in case the man got up and tried again.

When Leedy finally regained the power of speech, it did not occur to him to be grateful. "Where *were* you? You're supposed to be protecting me!"

"Thanks a lot, Leedy," grumbled the guard. He wondered if he wouldn't have been doing everybody a favor if he had been a couple of seconds late . . .

Route Seventy is a narrow strip of two-lane blacktop that cuts straight as an arrow through the heart of South Florida. The road is treacherous and the scenery comes in two types: swampland, which is green and flat, and dry land, which is brown and flat. Both types are ugly.

It's a good place for a prison and it's the kind of country where people actually vote in favor of bringing a federal prison to their district, figuring it will improve the quality of life and fatten up the tax base. Up until then the small towns along the way made only a modicum of money off speed traps, catching tourists attempting to spring from the Gulf Coast to the Atlantic without so much as a stop for gas or coffee or a tacky souvenir.

Terry and Pete Nessip were rarities on Route Seventy. They had business being there—to be sure, it was prison business—but they didn't like the look of the surroundings any more than any of the tourists did.

Pete Nessip, the older of the two brothers, drove the stripped down, no-air, no-radio, no-power-nothing kind of muddy brown Chevrolet Caprice, a car so unadorned that it could only belong to a government agency. His eyes were narrowed, half closed against the glare in the sky and the heat shimmer rising off the hot tar.

"Without the prison, alligator wrestling would be the biggest industry around here," he said.

His younger brother snorted scornfully and rolled his eyes. "You're avoiding the subject."

Pete nodded but never took his eyes off the road. "That's right. I am."

His brother threw his hands in the air as surrendering to the inevitable. "You're hopeless."

Pete nodded again. "That's right. I am."

Terry squirmed in his seat, unable to leave the topic there.

"But aren't you tired? Aren't you tired of two-month relationships?" He, unlike his brother, was a married man, and happily married to boot. Married people always thought they had the right—and the obligation—to give advice to their single friends. Sometimes, Pete got the feeling that Terry and his young wife, Cammie, were a little too interested in his matrimonial status. It was as if it was their hobby or something.

"You're just not meeting the right kind of woman, that's all."

"Yeah? And what kind of woman is that?" Pete glanced over at his brother. Both men were in their thirties, Pete older by a couple of years, and both were strong, athletically built men. They bore a strong physical resemblance, but the most obvious difference between the two—apart from temperament—was the deep scar that Pete had on the ridge of his left cheek, a ridge of broken flesh he carried as a souvenir of an accident on the firing range sustained during his time in the Army.

"You know . . ." Terry shrugged. "A woman who will

run with the wolves . . . Someone to keep you interested.''

'' 'Run with the wolves'?'' Pete laughed and shook his head, as if he couldn't quite believe what his little brother had said. ''I thought I warned you about watching too much Oprah.''

''All I'm saying is that a little excitement wouldn't kill you.''

''Forget it, I can't take those crazies. I like quiet women. Nice and dull. Not like that Mongolian feminist you fixed me . . .'' All of a sudden Pete knew where this was leading. And he had to put a stop to it early—because if he didn't, the next thing he knew, his brother would have arranged a date for him. If past history was any guide, a blind date arranged by his brother would certainly lead to public embarrassment, along with the definite possibility of unmitigated disaster. ''All right, who is she?''

''Who's who?'' said Terry, doing his best to feign innocence. ''Who are you talking about?''

''Don't give me that . . . Whenever we talk about my sex life it comes down to Cammie wanting to fix me up with some friend of hers. So, who is she?''

''Forget Cammie,'' Terry protested. ''Listen, this is your brother talking.''

''Who is she?''

Terry shrugged. ''Oh man, this is the thanks I get for being concerned about my big brother . . .''

They flashed by a large yellow and black sign at the side of the road: *Prison Area Next Three Miles. Do Not Stop. Do Not Pick Up Hitchhikers.*

''Almost there,'' said Pete.

''Now this . . . *this* is boring. Prisoner transport . . .''

10

Terry looked disgusted. "This is not what I joined the service for."

"I like it," said Pete smiling. "Nice and quiet. Just like my love life."

Both men were United States Marshals, federal agents working under the auspices of the Department of Justice. There were Marshals all over the United States, in every big city, in every federal courtroom; they sought fugitives from the law, enforced federal court orders and performed routine jobs like this one—transporting Earl Leedy to wherever the government wanted him transported.

Pete Nessip was the senior of the pair, having joined the US Marshals right after a three year hitch in the Army. It was the traditional path into the service, and when Terry had finished his tour in the Armed Forces, Pete brought him in, as if the Marshal's office was the family business. Of course, Pete felt responsible for Terry, the natural inclination of the older brother to look out for the younger, but when it came to Pete's sex life—or lack of it—Terry was the mother hen.

The concrete guard house of the Southland Federal Penitentiary appeared ahead and Pete slowed the car. "So what's her name?"

Terry grinned. "See, you *are* interested."

"No. It's just . . . Know your enemy."

"Like hell."

Pete stopped the car and leaned out of the window, flashing his marshal's badge at the guard. "Pete Nessip, Terry Nessip. United States Marshals."

The guard checked their names against a list on a clipboard, then waved them forward, the gates opening electronically as the Chevy nosed forward.

"So what's her name?"

"Shanandra," said Terry, as if his brother had tortured him into revealing some kind of deep dark secret. "Her name is Shanandra, okay?"

"Okay." They parked in the lot and Pete led the way into the main reception area of the prison. "Now that I know her name—keep her away from me."

The female corrections officer behind the thick shield of Plexiglas checked their IDs and badges and had them sign in.

"Any weapons, gentlemen?"

"Yeah," said Pete. They knew the drill. The brothers unclipped their waist holsters and handed over their standard issue sixteen-shot 9mm Berettas.

"Sign for them, please."

While Pete initialed the weapons log, Terry continued with the subject so dear to his heart. "Cammie's absolutely right, you know. You need someone bad, someone who—"

Pete looked at the female CO and shook his head. "This is my brother. He worries about me."

"Yeah," she commiserated. "Don't I know it. I get the same thing from my Mom."

"He's found some girl named Shanandra," said Pete.

"Shanandra? That's a pretty name."

"See?" said Terry.

"Sounds like a nightclub," Pete grumbled.

The guard slid two passes under the bulletproof barrier. "Down the hall. On the left, room 209."

"Thanks." Pete clipped the pass to the lapel of his suit coat and pushed on the armored door. The guard buzzed them in and they walked down the spartan hall toward the interrogation rooms in the prison's secure block.

There was a young man waiting for them in the office. He jumped to his feet as the two marshals entered. "Gordon Maples," he said, thrusting out his hand. "I'm with the United States Attorney's office."

"What do we have here?"

Maples motioned them into the interrogation room. "Take a look."

Through the glass they could see Earl Leedy slumped at one of the cheap prison issue Formica tables. His cats, Agnes and Cleo, gamboled at his feet.

"That's him?" asked Terry.

"That's him."

"What's his story?"

"The DEA began electronically seizing from offshore banks, so the Chang organization brought Leedy in as their computer hack. He kept the money moving so the DEA couldn't find it. Apparently it was quite a performance. No one knew how he did it. Turns out the bad guys have a better computer wonk than the good guys."

Terry and Pete peered through the glass, as if looking at an animal in the zoo.

"That guy in there coughing up fur balls is some kind of genius?" Terry sounded incredulous.

Maples nodded. "The best. He broke codes that can't be broken . . . it was like he lived inside the computers. He's got a personality to match, by the way."

"So how did he get caught?"

"His ego got in the way," said Maples. "He felt underappreciated. So he cut a deal with us to testify. For eighteen months we've hid him. Now two weeks from trial—they found him."

"Found him?" asked Pete. "What happened?"

"He got jumped in the yard. Day before yesterday. Leedy came real close to buying it."

"You sure Leedy didn't just piss this guy off at lunch?" Pete Nessip knew about prisons. They were pressure cookers where the slightest insult, the merest affront could result in a blood feud that didn't end until someone died.

"Maybe someone hated cats," Terry chimed in.

"No chance. Leedy has been separated from the population. Eats alone, showers alone. He was *supposed* to exercise alone, but someone came damn close to planting a shank in him."

"Who did it?"

"The guy who attacked him used to work for the Changs on the West coast. Obviously, someone got the word to him that Leedy had to go."

"So you want him moved?" said Terry.

"That's right," said Maples. "The government's got five million dollars and two years invested in this case. We need Mr. Leedy alive long enough to testify. That's *your* job."

The brothers exchanged a look, then they glanced through the window at Leedy.

"What about his cats?" asked Terry. "We don't have to take them, do we?"

"Yeah," said Pete. "We skipped the class where they covered cats."

"Very funny. Your task is to make Mr. Leedy as comfortable as possible. We want him to be . . . amenable."

"Isn't keeping him alive enough?" said Pete. "I would have thought he'd be grateful for that."

"Gentlemen, I think it's time you met Mr. Leedy . . ." said Maples, as if that would explain everything.

2

The Nessip brothers found they disliked Earl Leedy from the git go. Far from being appreciative that they sprung him from prison, Leedy complained and whined all the way across Florida. Griping endlessly during the long hot drive from the prison to the Metro Dade airport in Miami.

He moaned about the health of his cats, about the heat, about the discomfort of the handcuffs that he was required to wear, per standard procedure of the Marshal's service. At the outset, Pete and Terry did their best to placate their prisoner, but after a hundred miles of interminable argument, the Nessip brothers gave up and ignored him.

But that did not seem to deter Leedy. For mile after mile, he bitched and wailed and he was still at it when they drove onto the tarmac at the airport. Pete brought the car to a halt near a giant commercial 747 airliner.

Leedy gaped at the huge airplane, as if he had never seen one before. "What's that?"

Pete half turned in the seat. "What's it look like, Leedy?"

"I can't get on that."

"Shuttup." Pete turned to his brother. "You stay with him." He jerked a thumb over his shoulder. "I'm going to check things out."

15

"You always draw the easy duty." Terry unfolded a copy of that day's Miami Herald and studiously ignored his prisoner in the backseat.

"Why couldn't we take the train?" Leedy whined.

Terry scanned the front page of the newspaper and then turned to the sports section.

"I'm afraid to fly."

Terry did his best to look as if he was lost in the wonder of the National League box scores.

"I suffer from motion sickness and acrophobia. That's fear of heights, in case you didn't know."

His eyes never left the newspaper. Never before had the combined, dismal stats of the New York Mets roster seemed quite so fascinating.

"I may vomit," Leedy warned.

"*You* may vomit," Terry muttered.

Pete walked across the apron toward the plane, taking in the scene. Ground crews were swarming over the plane, teams busy fueling the craft, slinging meals into the galleys and loading luggage into the cavernous belly. Service rules required that Marshals look over any plane to be used for prisoner transport well before embarkation, searching for anything untoward, anything out of the ordinary that might suggest that the flight had been compromised. Like most procedures laid down in the manual, the visual inspection of the aircraft was nonsense—anyone intent on hijacking an airplane, blowing it up or otherwise interfering with a prisoner transfer would be unlikely to make a mistake so basic that it could be spotted easily.

Still, the rules were the rules, so Pete dutifully went about examining the undercarriage housing and watching as the bags were packed in the hold. One of the first pieces of baggage stowed was an outsized cat carrier.

Agnes and Cleo peered out through the plastic window, mewling pathetically.

He felt a tap on his shoulder. "US Marshal?"

Pete turned. "Yeah?"

"Norm Fox, Miami PD."

Nessip didn't ask for a badge or any other kind of ID—a cop could always tell another cop. "What can I do for you?"

"Justice asked us to give you a hand on this Leedy thing."

"Really?" Pete shook his head slowly. "This guy must really be important." In his ten years in the service, Pete had managed a hundred prisoner transfers—and not once had the Department of Justice asked the local police department to help out.

"From what I hear, he's worth his weight in gold," said Fox.

"Hard to believe." Pete glanced toward the car. He could see that Leedy was still jabbering away just as Terry continued to do his best to ignore him.

"Yeah, isn't it? You finished here?" He cocked his chin toward the baggage compartment.

"Yep. All we have to do is check out the interior of the plane and that's it."

The two cops walked through the main cabin of the aircraft, opening every overhead luggage compartment and carefully searching each of the three galleys. A cleaning crew was working its way down the aisle, vacuum cleaners thrumming on the carpet, while a maintenance worker was doing last minute repairs to a broken seat back. Fox stopped each in turn and checked their identification, while Pete Nessip walked the length of the plane from cockpit to tail, failing to detect anything out of the ordinary.

Nessip and Fox shrugged at each other. "Everything seems normal," said Fox.

"Okay," said Nessip. "Let's load 'em up."

It never failed to amaze Pete Nessip that so many people, carrying so much junk, could squeeze into the cramped confines of an airplane cabin and after a certain amount of floundering around, get it together to stow their gear and settle in seats.

The US Marshals and their prisoner were the first on the aircraft, Terry and Leedy sitting together—Leedy in the middle seat of a bank of three, Terry on the aisle; Pete was across the aisle. Earl Leedy shifted nervously in his seat, antsy and high-strung about the forthcoming flight. Pete and his brother had done this so many times before that flying held no terrors for them.

But they were alert, still on the job. Pete watched the passengers as they stumbled down the walkways, as they checked their boarding passes against the row numbers and put their carry-on bags in the overhead luggage compartments. None of the passengers excited any interest at all—if there were any terrorists or hijackers in the crowd, they were keeping themselves well disguised.

The only passenger of any interest held no threat—a ten year old girl, carrying a toy tiger almost as big as she was, came down the aisle, guided through the other people by an attractive flight attendant. It was obvious what was going on: the little girl was travelling alone, entrusted to the care of airline personnel.

The flight attendant—she wore a name tag which identified her as Norma—sat the little girl down in the seat directly in front of Pete.

"Here," Norma said to the little girl, "let me help you with your bags."

Lena nodded gravely. "Thank you."

Norma opened the luggage compartment above the seat and put away a couple of Lena's bags. In doing so, she dropped the stuffed tiger, hitting Pete in the face. But he grabbed it before it hit the ground.

"Ooops," she said. "Sorry."

"Hey, that's what I'm here for," Pete said, flashing her a smile. "Cat protection."

"Good thing, too," said Norma. "Are you okay, Lena?"

"Uh-huh."

"Good. I'll be back to check on you in a couple of minutes, okay?"

Terry and Pete watched as the stewardess walked back down the aisle.

Terry rolled his eyes at his brother. " 'That's what I'm here for . . .' Man, that's smooth." He left no doubt as to how lame he thought his brother's line.

"Gimme a break," Pete muttered.

"You're sure you fed them well?" asked Leedy. Cat protection was a subject very close to his heart.

Terry looked puzzled. "Fed? Fed who?"

"Agnes and Cleo, of course," said Leedy indignantly. "That's who."

"Oh. Yeah. Them."

"Agnes has low blood sugar."

Pete leaned across the aisle. "Agnes is better fed than we'll be on this flight, Leedy. Remember that."

"Excuse me . . ." A large man, beer belly hanging over his belt and enormous blue jeans riding low on his hips, leaned over Pete. He had the window seat in Pete's row. He squeezed by, but it was a tight fit.

Leedy refused to be placated. "Better fed than us? You're not just saying that?"

19

"No, Leedy," said Pete with a sigh. The sooner this job was over the happier he would be.

"How do we know the temperature will stay constant in the baggage compartment? They might freeze." He paled as the full weight of his words struck home. "Oh my God!"

"Leedy, I'm gonna kill both of your goddamn cats if you don't give it a rest," said Pete. "And what's more, I am going to see you not even around to bury the furry little creatures because you'll be in solitary. Got it?"

Pete winked at Terry, who did his best to stifle a laugh. But Leedy's jaw dropped, horror-struck at Pete's words.

"You wouldn't dare . . ." He gasped. "I'll sue. I'll sue you. I'll sue the United States Government . . ."

"Okay, Leedy," said Pete. "I've heard enough from you." He tapped the big man in the window seat on the shoulder. "Listen, how would you like an aisle seat? I'll switch with you."

The poor guy was squeezed into his seat and jammed up against the wall of the plane. "Hey, that would be great."

Pete shot a glance at Leedy. "The pleasure is all mine, believe me."

3

The passengers on the flight didn't know it, but things were not going well. After the obligatory standing on the runway, waiting for a long line of planes ahead of them to be cleared for takeoff, Flight 611 did get off the ground more or less on time. The big airliner attained its cruising altitude of thirty thousand feet about ten minutes after takeoff—but it didn't stay there long.

On the flight deck, the pilot and crew had been watching a storm system coming in off the Gulf, hoping that they could make a run to the north before the high winds and rain cut across the path of the 747. However, the storm had picked up speed in the last hour, and the leading edge of the weather system was beginning to buffet the aircraft.

The pilot contacted the Miami tower, asking for permission to climb, to fly up and over the turbulent weather. The plane was not in any real danger—747s were famous for the amount of abuse they could take—but storms slowed down air traffic and a rough flight upset the passengers.

Miami came back with permission in a matter of seconds and while the co-pilot put the craft into a computer assisted climb, the captain clicked on the intercom.

"We're getting some heavy weather folks," he said.

"So I've got permission to climb to 38,000 feet to see if we can get on top of it."

The passengers received this news in silence, few of them realizing that a steep climb over the bad weather would delay their flight considerably. But that was nothing—Flight 611 was about to get much worse.

The flight engineer was monitoring the radio, idly listening to the chatter in the corridor. There was a United Airliner a mile behind him, an American 737 a mile ahead and periodically they reported their radar contact points to their ground controllers. In a moment, it would be Flight 611's turn to do the same thing. But before the engineer could speak, Miami came up. The message was an urgent one and the Flight Engineer could feel a sharp bolt of fear as he listened.

He threw on the cockpit speaker. "Bob," he said to the pilot. "I think you better listen to this."

The voice of the Miami controller was grim. "611, this is Miami approach . . . we've just received an emergency transmission . . ."

In the main cabin, the flight attendants were finishing the start up service—drinks and little bags of peanuts—and were preparing to serve dinner.

Norma was walking down the aisles with two large bottles of wine, one red, the other white. No one noticed that she was offering it only to Pete, nor did anyone seem to observe that her smile seemed slightly strained, as if she was forcing herself to look happy.

"Wine?" She kept her voice low, not wanting to wake the large man who was sprawled in his seat, sound asleep.

Pete assumed that she was flirting with him, so he flirted right back. "Thanks," he said with a wink. "But I only drink wine by candlelight."

22

From across the aisle, Terry watched his brother, appalled at how clumsily Pete was handling himself. Banter with pretty girls had never been his brother's strong suit. "Jesus."

"I might be able to help you out then," said Norma. "Would you like to follow me?"

Peter couldn't quite believe his ears—and neither could Terry. As Pete got to his feet and squeezed past the sleeping bulk in the aisle seat, he smirked at his brother. "Home run on the first pitch," he whispered.

"Unbelievable," said Terry, watching his brother following Norma up the walkway. "Just unbelievable."

Leedy was fanning himself with the safety card from the seat pocket. "I think I'm going to be sick."

Terry nodded vigorously. "Yeah, I know what you mean. He makes me feel the same way."

Leedy looked panicky. He tossed aside the laminated card and pointed at the carpeted floor. "I'm not joking now, I can't relax. I think I can hear my little pussy cats crying down there."

"Leedy," Terry groaned. "Shut the fuck up."

Norma led Pete all the way to the front of the aircraft, past the galley just aft of the first class cabin, and stopped at the foot of the staircase that led upstairs to business class and the flight deck.

"What's this all about?"

Norma wasn't smiling now. "The captain needs to see you, right away. In the cockpit."

Pete took the steps two at a time. Whatever was going on, it couldn't be good.

The captain met Pete at the door of the cabin, grim faced. "We just received this."

The flight engineer put a tape up on the cockpit intercom. There was a moment of static, then a voice: "Flight 611 out of Miami is about to be taken over by the Posse Commitus. Stay on your flight plan and no one will be hurt. You will receive further instructions in five minutes . . ."

"When did this come in?"

"Two minutes ago," said the captain.

Pete pulled his Beretta from his waist holster, clicked off the safety catch and chambered a round. "Has the FBI been contacted?"

The pilot nodded. "First thing."

"Let them know there are two US Marshals on board," he said, as he slipped the gun back into its holster. "I'm going back down there."

There were five of them—four men and one woman—and they were scattered around the cabin, waiting for the signal to begin the attack.

Furthest forward, on the left side of the side of the plane was Torski. He was about thirty-five years old. Tall, balding, thin as a whip. He had a small smudge of moustache, a nasty smile and fancied himself a cowboy—he wore a Texas long horn earring in the lobe of his right ear.

Torski's best friend, Deputy Dog, seated a few rows behind, was a small, slender Oklahoman. He had pale blue eyes and a mean streak a mile wide.

Near to Deputy Dog was the only woman in the group, Kara. She was a tough looking woman from Duluth, Minnesota. She had been raised on the mean streets of the city, down on the waterfront of Lake Superior and although she was the youngest member of the team, years of hard living showed in her face—and she was just as ruthless and cruel as any of the men.

Jagger didn't quite fit in with the rest of the group, a contract player, more stable and less violent than the rest. He was in his early forties, good looking, with dark devilish eyes and a deep scar that jagged across his left cheek, a souvenir of an old knife fight.

At the very rear of the plane was Ty Moncrief, the leader of the team. He was supremely self-confident, absolutely sure of his skills and his abilities.

It was Moncrief who started the ball rolling. He ripped open the back of the seat in front of him—it was the seat that maintenance man had been repairing prior to takeoff—revealing a secret compartment stuffed with automatic weapons and grenades. He grabbed oxygen masks from the carry-on bag at his feet just as Kara and Torski jumped up and rolled smoke grenades down the passageways. In an instant, the cabin was filled with a pall of thick gray smoke. People began screaming.

Deputy Dog had a gun in his hand. "This is a hijacking! Get your heads down!"

Torski was spinning forward, cutting through the smoke. He had a vest full of plastic explosives strapped to his chest. "Nobody move or we blow this plane out of the sky!"

"Eyes down!" Ty Moncrief ordered.

Panic gripped the passengers, many of them throwing themselves to the floor. Terry stayed in his seat. Instinctively, his hand dropped to his gun—but he didn't dare shoot. He could hardly see through the smoke and he still had no sense of how many hijackers there were on board.

"Everyone remain calm and no one will get hurt!" The barrel of Ty's gun swept over the passengers. It was time to get some respect. The gun settled on the big man sitting in Pete's aisle seat. He was looking up nervously.

"I said, eyes down." Without further warning, Moncrief fired twice, the bullets slamming into the man's chest, killing him instantly.

This time Terry reached for his gun, but he only managed to get it half out of his holster before Ty nailed him with a shot to the chest. Terry slumped forward in his seat, mortally wounded. Leedy was going berserk with fear, screaming and whimpering.

Ty Moncrief yanked Leedy out of his seat and jammed the gun against his teeth. "Anyone else move and I'll kill this passenger. Heads down!"

All heads went down, all eyes fixed to the floor or clenched tight. People were praying . . .

Ty passed Leedy to the rear of the plane, Torski grabbing him and hustling him toward the rear exit door. Kara was at the door, setting small explosive charges on the lock and hinges.

"Okay!" yelled Ty to his group. "Let's move it! Now!" He went racing down the aisle toward the rear of the aircraft. As he passed, Terry found the strength to raise his gun and fire once. The bullet hit home, staggering the big man—but he was wearing a bulletproof vest.

"I warned you," he said, raising his gun.

But before he could squeeze off a shot, Pete ran and dove through the smoke, smashing into Ty Moncrief like a linebacker. Right then, the explosive charges on the door detonated, the emergency door ripping away from the body of the aircraft and hurtling into the black air.

The pressure inside the cabin dropped instantaneously—the screams of the passengers were overpowered by the shrill shriek as the depressurized air rushed through the cabin. Passengers were hurtling toward the opening, screaming as they were sucked out of the aircraft and into the void. The overhead compartments slammed open and luggage shot through the air to the opening. A service cart flew down the aisle and smashed into Ty and Pete, before blasting out the back of the plane like a cannonball, slamming off into space.

The force of impact separated the two men, Ty slipping from Pete's grasp. Pete hooked his legs around a seat stanchion and held on, the force of the pressure pulling him toward the jagged opening.

Lena's stuffed tiger rushed by him, the little girl herself was being pulled from her seat, the power of the rushing wind literally jerking her right out of her shoes. Pete watched in horror as Lena flew down the aisle and slammed into Jagger, clutching for a handhold. She grabbed at him, clawing away his oxygen mask. For a moment, she could see his face, the face of Rasputin come to life. The twisted scar on his cheek seemed to glow red on his contorted face.

Jagger tore himself free and pushed the mask back on to his face. He scrambled to his feet and vanished into the smoke. The instant he let go of Lena, the little girl began sliding quickly toward the opening—but just before she vanished into the black abyss a hand reached out and grabbed her. It was Terry using the last of his fast-ebbing strength, to stop the little girl from being sucked out of the airplane.

Pete knew that his brother wouldn't be able to hang on for long. He inched his way down the aisle and reached out for his brother, grabbing him around the ankle.

"Hang on, Terry," he gasped. "Hang on . . ."

With all this strength Terry pulled Lena away from the gap and toward his brother. Pete stretched and grasped the child, hauling her away from the gap and passing her over his shoulder to Norma. The minute the little girl was safe, Terry's grip began to falter. Pete felt it instantly.

"No . . . Goddamnit, Terry. Hold on."

But Terry was beginning to slip from Pete's grasp. He looked his brother in the eye. Terry showed no signs of panic, but he seemed to know that he couldn't hang on.

"You can do it, Terry." Pete spoke through clenched teeth. "Hold on." As Terry's clutch weakened, Pete grabbed for the sleeve of his jacket, but the material started to tear almost immediately. With a last effort, Pete lunged and tried to grab his brother, but Terry was torn away and flung into the dark night.

4

From the moment the door had blown, the crew on the flight deck had been battling to save the plane. The nose went down and the pilot put the aircraft into a steep dive, trying to get to a lower altitude as fast as possible. Every alarm in the cabin was sounding, the computer screens glitched out in a shower of green static. The pilot worked feverishly, shutting down all computer systems, taking physical control of the craft.

The flight engineer had found a possible landing site, a small country airport near Deltona. The runway was too short for a 747, but it was better than trying to put down in a field or a swamp—and there was absolutely no chance that they would make it to the only large airport in the area at Jacksonville.

The plane had lost almost thirty thousand feet of altitude in a matter of minutes. At ten thousand feet, the pilot threw the plane into a sharp bank, slowing the craft.

"Shut down all electrical systems!" the pilot ordered. "Vent fuel! Spark damper on!"

A great gout of liquid streamed from the wing tanks, showering the ground with aviation fuel. The plane was light and as stable as could be expected at five thousand feet. It was going to be a dead stick landing, an ungainly belly flop onto the ground.

"Everything off. Shut down the engines!"

The four jet engines died. The air was filled with the screams of the passengers and the wail of tortured metal. The plane hit the ground tail first and plowed through the soft earth for a hundred yards before coming to a halt.

For Pete, the next few minutes passed in a blur. The cabin was filled with smoke and fire, the cries of the injured and the panic-stricken. He helped where he could, throwing open one of the emergency exits and inflating the slide and assisting people off the plane. It was only when emergency services began to arrive that he remembered that his brother was dead . . .

By midnight, the whole scene had been overrun by rescue workers and Federal Aviation Agency investigators. Last to arrive was Tom McCracken of the US Marshal's office—Pete's immediate superior. As he crossed the crash sight he was stopped by two FBI men, agents called in to secure the area.

"Who are you?" one of them demanded.

McCracken flashed his badge. "Tom McCracken—US Marshal's office. Who are *you*?"

"Glenn Blackstone, agent in charge, FBI." He pointed to his companion. "Bob Covington."

"I'm looking for my guy, Pete Nessip."

The two FBI agents exchanged glances. "He's over there," said Blackstone. "I think you should know that some of the survivors say that one of your guys may have caused this . . ."

McCracken stopped dead in his tracks. "What? What the hell are you talking about? Pete Nessip wouldn't—"

"Not him," said Blackstone. "The other one. Survivors say the other brother opened fire, hit the hijacker carrying explosives and that blew the plane."

"That's bullshit," said McCracken flatly.

The FBI agents thought that McCracken sounded awfully positive for someone who just showed up at the scene.

"Maybe he thought he had a clean shot," said Covington. "Maybe he panicked"—he shrugged—"who knows what happened up there?"

"Panicked? My marshals don't panic. Especially these two guys."

"Well," said Covington. "Bottom line is he made a mistake and fourteen people are dead."

"Yeah?" muttered McCracken. "We'll see about that . . ." He strode toward Pete, the two FBI agents trailing behind him.

Pete sat slumped on the damp ground, his face a study in heartsick anguish. His eyes were vacant, hollow, scarcely seeing the smoking ruin of the plane or the activities of the rescue workers who were carrying away the injured, loading them on to one of dozens of ambulances.

McCracken put his hand on his agent's shoulder. "What did you see, Pete. Did you see *anything*?"

Pete Nessip shrugged. "There were two men, maybe more. I didn't see their faces. There was so much smoke . . . confusion."

"You didn't hear them say anything?"

"No," Pete whispered. "There was a little girl and I was trying to hold her. And my brother. He was hurt . . . I was trying to get him back . . ."

Pete was so deep in his agony, that McCracken and the two FBI agents just stood in silence.

"Terry had been shot," said Pete after a moment. His voice was low and shaky. "Shot bad . . . He lost a lot of blood. But I couldn't hold him. I couldn't . . . hold him." He closed his eyes, but in the darkness he could see his brother's face as he slipped from his grasp and into the deadly night.

The FAA-FBI investigation into the crash of Flight 611 began immediately, that night. Survivors were still being pulled from the wreckage, but investigative teams had moved into the few small buildings of the airfield, laying down additional phone lines and installing powerful computer work stations.

The FBI agents, Covington and Blackstone, were huddled over one screen, watching an employee of the airline log into the data on Flight 611. McCracken stood back a bit, glancing nervously at Pete Nessip, who sat still and dazed, as though in shock.

"Bring up the passenger list and seat assignments," Blackstone ordered.

"Yes, sir." The airline rep's fingers flew over the keyboard. Data began scrolling across the keyboard.

"Break out the ticket purchases, separate them into credit card and cash." Blackstone knew that the hijackers were more likely to have paid cash for their seats, rather than with easy-to-trace credit cards. "Then cross-check with advance reservations and same day purchase."

"Uh-huh." The full list of passengers had appeared on the screen, then a series of figures, coded numbers which indicated where and when the seat had been booked and the method of payment used.

A second after the data appeared on the screen the names and numbers began flashing, then one by one they began to disappear. The numbers went wild, rearranging and jumbling, the information scattering and vanishing, like leaves blowing off a tree.

"What the hell are you doing?" Covington demanded.

The airline rep shrugged. "Nothing. It's some kind of virus or worm, sir."

"Well, make it stop!"

"I'm trying, but the whole system is going down." He pounded the keys of his computer, trying to reverse the deterioration of the information on the screen.

All of the terminals in the room were beginning to lock up and scramble. Electronic information was being devoured right before their eyes—and they were powerless to stop it.

"What is this?" said Blackstone. "System overload? When can you get it back?"

The airline clerk looked dubious. "This seems to be a little more serious than a simple system glitch." In fact, the man had never seen data just vanish like that before— once a computer forgot something, it stayed forgotten.

It did not look like it, but Pete Nessip had been listening to the activity around him. As the computers in the room began to seize up and shut down, in Pete's mind things were beginning to come clear, the big picture was beginning to emerge.

"Leedy," he said.

Covington shot him a look. "What?"

"Leedy . . . He's a computer genius and—" His mind was working fast now. "It was a setup. The whole thing was a setup."

"A *what*?" demanded Covington.

"Don't you see—"

Blackstone folded his arms across his chest and glared at Pete. "What the hell are you saying, Nessip? A prison break at thirty thousand feet?"

"Why not?"

"Oh come on, Pete," said Covington. "Use your

head. What did they do? Come and pick him up in a spaceship."

"Look," said Pete. "I tackled one of the guys. He was wearing some kind of pack. Maybe a parachute."

"Sure," said Blackstone skeptically. "What about Leedy? What did he do, open an umbrella and float down like Mary Poppins? Nobody saw any parachutes."

"Of course not," Pete replied. "People were scared to death. Their heads were down, and the plane was full of smoke. Nobody would have seen anything."

"What thirty-two people *did* see was your brother fire at a man wrapped in explosives," said Blackstone. "That's a fact."

"That's a lie."

"Pete . . ." McCracken cautioned. "Take it easy."

But Pete was in no mood to be reined in. "What's going on here? Does the FBI give a bonus for how fast you wrap up a case? Is that it? We're talking about my brother. Isn't it worth investigating?"

Covington shook his head. "You want an investigation? You want facts? How about this—two hours after the explosion, an airline maintenance man was shot dead at Miami airport while running from a detective."

"So?"

"So his apartment was full of Posse Commitus literature," said Blackstone. "Not to mention enough homemade C-4 plastic explosive to blow up a dozen airliners."

"He planted explosives on board?" asked McCracken. "That explains how they got the stuff through airport security."

"Not only that, but the Miami PD detective on the scene—Fox—remembered the guy from the pre-flight inspection. He was repairing a seat and we figure that he hid the weapons and the explosives."

"Look, Nessip . . ." said Covington. "I'm sorry about your brother. Nobody wants to paint him as a fall guy, but if he hadn't panicked and opened fire, fourteen people wouldn't be dead."

"My brother didn't panic," he said. Pete shot the two agents a look so cold it could freeze them in their tracks. The certainty in his voice was almost enough to convince every man in the room.

One of the FAA investigators tapped Covington on the shoulder. "Sir . . . Forensics just got a positive ID from one of the remains. It was the prisoner, Leedy."

Pete was stunned into silence by this revelation. Covington and Blackstone looked triumphant—as far as they were concerned, that piece of information iced Pete's theory. Even McCracken's faith in Pete suddenly splintered.

5

By dawn the next morning, the FAA and the FBI investigators had decided that they had enough information on the crash of Flight 611 to face the media. All night long microwave transmission trucks had been trundling up the road to the crash site and reporters had been clamoring for some word on the causes of the accident.

It was Covington who stepped up to the microphones flanked by Blackstone as well as a throng of local cops and a brace of FAA investigators.

"Through massive efforts by Federal, State and local law enforcement officials," said Covington, "the FBI believes it has answered most of the questions concerning the attempted hijacking of Flight 611 . . ."

The instant he paused, the press started shouting questions. "Passengers said there was a United States Marshal on board who caused the explosion—"

Covington held up his hands for silence. "The primary cause of the explosion and the deaths of the passengers was the overzealous action of a US Marshal who was armed and on board the plane . . ."

CNN was carrying this news conference live. A couple of hundred miles to the south Ty Moncreif and his team were clustered around a TV set on his boat watching intently.

"They're buying it!" shouted Deputy Dog exultantly. "They're buying it top to bottom."

Ty Moncrief's eyes did not leave the set, completely focused on the action on the screen. "Of course they're buying it. That's the way I planned it."

The scheme had been almost letter perfect. After bailing out of the plane, the terrorist team had picked up its transport and beat south fast. Their headquarter-hideout was a dilapidated fishing shack, a rundown building standing on rickety stilts in the middle of a trackless swamp. The only way in or out was by boat; their electricity came from their own generator, although lines from the South Florida power grid were strung across a portion of the desolate swamp.

Torski still hadn't come down from the elation of pulling off the daring hijacking. "Man, what a rush, huh? When we went out of that plane that wind hit me like a fuckin' express train."

Jagger laughed. "I'm tracking away from the plane and suddenly I'm face-to-face with some lady still holding a magazine!"

Ty glanced into the house. "Leedy done throwing up yet?"

Kara dragged Earl Leedy out of the house. The computer genius was in a total frenzy, pacing nervously, his Adam's apple bobbing up and down like a fishing float. His hand was wrapped in a bandage and his face was drained of color.

"Christ! Oh, Christ!" he said bouncing around on the porch of the house. "My hand!"

"Shut up and thank me," said Ty icily.

"Thank you!" Leedy screeched. "You threw me out of an airplane. You cut off my finger!"

"How many do you need? You've still got nine left.

And you crashed the airline computer system with one hand didn't you?'' Ty turned back to the television set. The press conference had come to an end and a TV reporter was doing a wrap-up from the crash site. He was standing in front of the wrecked plane.

"The marshal, whose name is being withheld, fired at a hijacker and set off the explosion which killed fourteen people, including the hijackers, a group calling themselves the Posse Commitus . . .''

Leedy stopped pacing and blinked several times rapidly. The plan was beginning to make sense to him. "They think I'm dead? That means I'm free.''

Ty smiled thinly. "Leedy, as of now I own your ass and what's left of your hands. But you have nothing to worry about—I'm going to make this all worth your while.''

Leedy didn't like the sound of this at all. His smile vanished in a flash. "What about the other marshal?''

"He's dead,'' said Ty. "I shot him.''

"I don't think so. He was in the john.''

Ty shrugged. "Then all he saw was smoke. We all got out clean—except for that little bitch who grabbed Jagger.'' He turned his icy stare on Jagger. "Why didn't you throw her out the door?''

Jagger shifted uncomfortably. "I—I didn't think it was necessary. She didn't see anything. I'm sure of it.''

"I hope not,'' said Moncrief, standing up. "For your sake . . .'' He nodded at Kara. "Let's get going. We have a lunch date.''

It was proof of Ty Moncrief's astonishing powers of endurance that he could pull off the daring jailbreak on Flight 611 at night and appear at a chic Miami restaurant for lunch a few hours later. He was clear-eyed and relaxed, looking as if he had done nothing more strenuous than get a good night's sleep.

Of course, it wasn't a lunch he would have missed for anything. The object of this whole exercise—the hijacking, grabbing Leedy—was to make money, pure and simple. And the two men that Ty and Kara were meeting in Miami were representatives of a man with very deep pockets.

Walsh Mathews was the senior of the two men, both in age and authority. Schuster Stevens was the sidekick, constantly talking on a cellular phone, in continual contact with his shadowy employer.

All through lunch, Mathews and Stevens had listened to Ty Moncrief's effective and rather persuasive sales pitch. When he had finished, Stephens excused himself, pulled out his cellular phone, excused himself and went to place his call.

He returned a few minutes later. "Good news, Mr. Moncrief," he said, smiling slightly. "Our client finds your offer quite . . . interesting."

"But he's troubled by the fact that you used to be an agent for the Drug Enforcement Agency."

Ty shrugged. " 'Used to be' is exactly why I am worth something to him."

Mathews and Stevens glanced at each other—Ty Moncrief could tell by their looks that his words had hit home. The two men knew that if the commodity he was selling was credible it could be worth a fortune to their boss.

"But why should he trust you?" Stephens asked.

"He's not going to," said Ty. "And I won't trust him." He leaned forward slightly and lowered his voice. "But what I'm offering him no one else in the world can provide. Remember that."

"Are you sure of that?" asked Mathews.

"Of course. And to prove it I'm going to give him a little taste. For free. Just this once."

"Very generous," said Stevens.

"You think? The next time we meet," said Moncrief, "tell him to bring his big fat wallet." He stood up and took Kara's hand. "Thanks for the lunch guys . . ."

The turnout for Terry Nessip's funeral was thin, just his family, a few friends and a couple of US Marshals. It was as if Terry's memory could contaminate, taint the mourners with the guilt that he was carrying to his grave.

Pete stood next to Terry's widow, Cammie, his hand resting on the shoulder of his nephew, Terry's son, five-year-old Taylor. Both were doing their best to bear up under the strain of their grief. Taylor, of course, had little idea of what was going on, but he knew that his mother and his uncle were sad, so he was sad too.

As Terry had been a serving member of the US Marshal's service who died in the line of duty, there was a little pro-forma ceremony. There was a flag draped over his casket, and when the coffin had been lowered into the ground, the flag was carefully folded up and handed to Cammie—as if a few feet of red, white and blue cloth would make up for all that had happened to her and her family.

McCracken, Pete, and Cammie walked away from the grave site at the conclusion of the funeral. The few other mourners dispersed quickly, as if they might be faintly embarrassed to be seen there.

"I live in the same place all my life," said Cammie, watching the mourners leave. "One day my husband dies . . . and it's like I never knew anyone."

"He died doing his job, Cam," said McCracken. "That would have mattered to him."

Cammie fixed a steady gaze on McCracken. "Then why doesn't anybody say that?"

McCracken realized that there was nothing he could say to her, nothing that would make her feel better about the sudden, awful death of her husband. He kissed her lightly on the cheek. "I'm sorry," he said. "Call me if you need anything, okay?"

Cammie nodded. But they both knew that she would never ask for the Service's help.

Pete and Cammie watched him walk away.

"People come up to me in the grocery store and tell me he killed those people playing hero. I can't turn on the TV without someone saying it was his fault." Now it was Pete's turn to come under her determined eyes. "I want to know, Pete. Was it his fault?"

"No," he said.

"Then why do they say it?"

"They just need a way to explain it," said Pete softly. "They don't know what else to do."

The strain was beginning to overcome her ability to maintain her calm. Tears welled into her eyes.

"Well, that's just great," she said, her voice tight. She bent and picked up her son, gathering him into her arms as if—suddenly, irrationally—she was afraid that he too would be taken from her.

She held her son close, Taylor burying his face in the crook of her neck.

"Who's going to explain it all to him?" she asked angrily. In that moment she hated her brother-in-law, hated the macho ethic that had driven her husband to risk his life in defense of strangers. She didn't trust herself to say any more. Cammie walked quickly to her car, holding her son close.

Pete watched her go, then turned and walked back to

the grave site. He stood on the freshly turned earth and watched as his brother's coffin was slowly lowered into the ground. Tears came to his eyes and the pain of his grief and the guilt that stayed with the living churned inside of him.

6

Sometime during the next few days, Pete dropped out of sight. He was on administrative leave following the death of his brother, a hiatus dictated by US Marshal Service regulations, but even if he hadn't been given a few days off, he would have taken them. He had work—real work—to do.

Pete was consumed by a single thought, the burning desire to prove that his brother had not panicked, that Terry was not responsible for the plane crash and the death of the innocent victims on board. He locked himself in his apartment, threw himself on the couch in the living room and lost himself in thought.

Pete proceeded from the assumption that the hijackers were not Posse Commitus. The Posse were old enemies of the US Marshal's Service, a radical fringe group dedicated to destroying the federal government. Pete knew them—they didn't have the know-how or the manpower to pull off a stunt like the taking of Flight 611. In addition, they usually operated out of the mid- and far West; he had never heard of them mounting any maneuvers in the southern or eastern parts of the country. In any case, if it *was* the Posse Commitus, he had no doubt that the US Marshals were rousting known members and sympathizers from western Pennsylvania all the way to the Pacific Ocean.

But Pete could feel it in his bones, he was sure that the hijackers were using the PC as cover. The real target was Earl Leedy and his wondrous computer skills—it never occurred to Pete that anyone would have gone through all of the trouble of grabbing Earl Leedy because they liked or admired him. No, someone needed the service that only that pain in the neck Earl Leedy could provide. For the time being, Pete put aside the question of why, and turned to the more pressing question of *how*.

He knew how they got the weapons—they were concealed in the phony seat back—but there wasn't enough room in that pouch to hide five, possibly six, high altitude parachute rigs. Somehow, they had managed to sneak the equipment they needed through airport security. The square badges, as cops called security guards, who manned the X-ray machines and metal detectors at the nation's airports did their job as well as they could, but there was no doubt in anyone's mind that they could be fooled if people were determined to do it. Still, *five* parachutes? Pete didn't know the first thing about skydiving—why jump out of a perfectly good airplane?—but he assumed that the harnesses and other parts of the rig must have metal parts, pieces that would have tripped the alarms at the airport security checkpoints.

The next question was where. Once they jumped they had to have landed somewhere and an outfit as daring as the group who had taken over Flight 611 would have planned well in advance where they would touch down. They would have had transport waiting. They would have planned for every contingency. How many places could there be within the flight path of Flight 611 that met all their requirements?

Pete left his house once in the next three days. He went downtown and did some shopping, hitting a couple of big bookstores and a computer software outlet, buying the research tools he needed to develop his theory.

When he got back to his apartment, he sat down at his computer, and didn't stand up again for eight hours. He was giving himself a crash course in skydiving, learning the ropes as best he could. Logging on to the Internet, he searched the mysterious back roads of the electronic world, searching among the arcane and recondite subject matter until he found a jumpers' forum. There he sat, downloading information and eavesdropping on the conversations—most of them spoken in a jargon as impenetrable as a foreign language. What were Vector tandem instructors? Or twelve steppers? Pack volume? Aspect ratio? There was a forest of acronyms—APS, AFF, I/JM, TRAC, FJC, IPC and more. . . .

For example, when the subject of HALO came up, it took him about forty-five minutes before he figured out that it was an acronym for "High Altitude, Low Opening . . ." It was just the kind of dangerous, specialized jump he wanted to know more about. He opened the video window in his computer and watched, mesmerized by images of hot-dog skydivers deploying their chutes at various altitudes.

But there was so much more he wanted to know—so much he *needed* to know. But he didn't ask any questions, like a stranger at a cocktail party, or a new kid in class, he was afraid of opening his mouth for fear that he would be laughed at and closed out of the source of information.

Pete's eyes hurt from the strain of staring at his video display terminal and his back ached from being hunched at the computer. Then he realized, with a shock, that night had fallen and he had been working without thought to time for hours on end.

He crashed for an hour or two, throwing himself down on the bed fully clothed, falling asleep in a matter of seconds. But his sleep was agitated and unsettled, as if his brain would not let him rest, forcing him to open his eyes and return to the urgent task at hand.

Included in his shopping spree were three maps of Florida: one was an ordinary gas station map of the state; more valuable to him was a topographical map issued by the United States Geological Survey, a plan so detailed it seemed to show every rise, every patch of swamp, every bump in the road; the third was a detailed map of the entire county.

He tacked all three of them to the wall and studied them like a general plotting a campaign. On all three maps he marked the point where the plane had come down, then, working backwards, he plotted the place where he thought the hijacking commenced. The landing site for the terrorists was, therefore, somewhere between those two positions.

Then, using what he had learned from the Internet and what his own training told him about surveillance and secrecy, he examined the county map looking for possible landing points. He found several.

The next step was to visit them and look for physical evidence. But before he could do that, there was a knock at his door. . . .

Pete had not only lost track of time, he had forgotten to eat, shave, even change his clothes. He was rumpled, red-eyed and he had thick growth of stubble on his chin. When McCracken appeared at his apartment that morning, he thought it looked as if Pete had been on a three-day drinking binge.

McCracken shook his head when he saw Nessip, feeling bad that a man could slip so low, so fast. It made the news he had come to deliver that much more cruel—but seeing Pete like this McCracken knew that it made sense too.

"I need to talk to you, Pete. It's important."

"So is this," Pete said. "Wait'll you see what I found." Pete was glad to see his chief at his door. He led McCracken into the house, talking excitedly as he went. He was so full of his idea, so convinced he was right, he didn't realize how he sounded—not just excited, but delirious, manic, wild—a man on the edge of some kind of breakdown.

Pete led McCracken through the disorder of his small apartment, straight to his wall of maps. He pounded the country map with his fist.

"Look at this," said Pete, his eyes glittering. "I got it nailed within two square miles where the hijackers must have landed. All we've got—"

"All we've got, Pete—" said McCracken cutting him off. "All we've got are bodies."

Pete nodded vigorously. "Yeah, yeah, I know. Don't you think it's a little weird that the only bodies burned beyond recognition were those of the terrorists and that little prick Leedy? That's a little too coincidental, too neat, wouldn't you say?"

McCracken knew why Pete was doing this—he couldn't imagine how hard it must be to see your own brother die and then have him blamed for deaths of innocent people. Pete was clutching at straws, trying anything, no matter how outlandish, to expiate the guilt and spread the blame.

"Pete," said McCracken as gently as he could. "No

one jumps from a 747 at that speed and that altitude and lives. It can't be done. Period.''

But McCracken couldn't dissuade Pete that easily. He grabbed a handful of papers, the fruits of his research, and waved them under his boss's nose. ''Wrong. A Navy SEAL team trained in a 727 three years ago. How about that? We've been set up, Tom. Don't you get it? The thing we need to figure is what they wanted Leedy for in the first place.''

McCracken was no longer listening. He was staring at the work—the obession—scattered all around him. The desk was cluttered with notebooks full of Pete's scribblings, crude drawings of the interior of a 747, piles of books and video stacked everywhere. This was not good—and McCracken was surprised. He would have figured that Pete Nessip would have been the last person to flip out.

For the first time, Pete saw the concern in McCracken's face. ''What? What is it? What are you doing here, anyway?''

''A board of review, Pete,'' said McCracken. ''That's why I'm here.''

''Board of review? What for?''

McCraken nodded. ''To determine responsibility. Yours and Terry's as regards the accident . . . It was bound to happen Pete, you must have known that. Please—don't take it personally.''

But there was no way Pete could do anything but take it to heart. ''Responsibility? Man, that some *bullshit* and you know it!''

McCracken was getting tired of placating Pete Nessip. It was time that his agent faced up to things. ''I know it, Pete? No, here's what I know: I know that the FAA and the airline are in the middle of a shit storm from the media, the insurance companies and relatives of the dead passengers. Nobody wants to hear about super terrorists grabbing computer geniuses and skydiving from 747s.''

''But if I can prove—''

McCracken held up his hands, as if fighting off Pete's words. ''Damn it, Pete, let me finish! No one is interested in what you can or cannot prove. No one cares, understand? Right now all anyone wants to do is point fingers—and they are pointing right at you and Terry. Okay?'' McCracken paused, the next part would be the hardest. ''So, you know the standard operating procedure on this . . . I have to ask for your badge and your gun.''

Pete was going to protest, but then thought the better of it. McCracken didn't want to do this but he had to, it was his job. There was no point in putting him through hell when he wasn't the enemy. Pete burrowed into a desk drawer and pulled out his gun, his badge, and his wallet ID.

''I'm not quitting on this,'' said Pete.

McCracken took the gun and badge and put them in the pocket of his suit coat. ''Pete, give it up. You can spend your whole life trying to make something different, but in the end, you can't really change it. What's happened—has happened. Now you have to live through it and put it behind you . . .''

Pete shook his head. ''Seeing as you've got my gun and badge I guess I'm not coming back to work anytime soon.''

McCracken nodded. ''The administrative leave is extended until after the board of review has made all of its determinations.''

''Well,'' said Pete with a thin smile. ''I think I know how I'm going to spend my summer vacation.''

McCracken knew that there were few things more disruptive and futile than an agent running around on his own time trying to prove a private theory. "Want some advice? Rest up. Go to the beach. Relax."

"Yeah, Tom," said Pete. "Whatever you say . . ."

Pete watched McCracken walk down to his car, then waited until he drove away. Then he slid open a drawer in his desk and pulled out another 9mm Beretta. He checked the chamber and then slapped in a clip, all ready for use when the time came.

The big hole in Pete's theory was the jump itself. As soon as he started talking about a bunch of hijackers skydiving from a commerical jet liner at almost forty thousand feet, people were going to ignore everything he said. He had to find out if it was possible and to get that information he went to the only people who had ever attempted anything similar—the Navy SEALS.

Pete knew there was a SEAL base down in the Florida Keys someplace, but they didn't exactly advertise their presence. It took him the better part of the next morning to get the Navy to admit that there was a post down there and to dig out of them the name of the public information officer for the base. The rest was relatively simple. Pete called the officer, identified himself as a US Marshal and asked for permission to visit the base. The PIO called the Marshal's office in Miami, confirmed that Pete was telling the truth about his identity, and issued a pass. No one—certainly not Pete—thought to tell the Department of the Navy that Pete Nessip was in very deep hot water. . . .

SEALS are trained in all manner of parachute maneuvers, but few of them had the varied experience of the commander Pete was lucky enough to connect with. They met at the foot of the parachute training tower.

"Commander?" said Pete, thrusting out his hand. "Pete Nessip, US Marshal's office."

"Hey Pete . . . Don't call me Commander, makes me feel old. Call me Dejaye." He was a wiry, hard-looking man, smaller than Pete would have guessed for one of the fabled Navy elite.

"Okay . . ."

"What's up?" He glanced at the enormous wristwatch strapped to his wrist, as if letting Pete know that his time was limited.

"I need to know if a team of skydivers could jump out of a commercial airliner. . . ."

"How high?"

"Thirty-eight thousand feet," said Pete. Suddenly, he felt foolish to be asking such a stupid question.

Dejaye considered the information. "I took a team out of a commercial jet. It was a Delta Squad hostage drill. Let me tell you, it's not easy and I wouldn't like to do it again, not if I didn't have to."

"So it *can* be done," Pete insisted. "It's not stretching too much. . . ."

Dejaye stopped and looked hard at Pete. "This is about that 747, isn't it? The one that came down the other day."

Pete nodded. "Yeah."

"That's a whole different ballgame, Pete. From what I read in the paper I would guess that conditions on board that flight were not . . . ideal." He smiled wryly. "Am I right?"

"You might say that. But when you took your team out of the 727 . . ."

"We did it," said Dejaye. "But it was a 727. It was

51

flying at twenty thousand feet. It was a drill. No one was shooting at us, no smoke, no passengers, no explosions. And even then it wasn't easy. A 747 at thirty-eight thousand feet?'' He shoot his head slowly. ''I dunno. . . .''

''But there's a chance it could be done?''

''You could try. The odds on success—not great.'' He thought a moment. ''Plus you've got another problem. Where did they get the chutes from in the first place?''

''I've thought about that,'' said Pete. ''I can't figure out how they got them on board.''

''Let me show you something. . . .'' Dejaye led him across the tarmac to a hangar. Inside men were working at long, wide tables, carefully folding and packing yards of brightly colored fabric into parachute packs.

Dejaye picked up one of the open chute packs and showed it to Pete. ''See these?'' The SEAL commander fingered one of the circles of metal that held the rig together. ''These D rings are high density metal. Your terrorists may have had someone stash a few guns behind a seat, but not five parachute rigs. And five rigs going through X-ray and metal detectors would raise holy hell with airport security.''

Pete nodded. ''I know, I know. I've been over that ground already.''

''And what did you figure out? How did they do it? I'd be interested to know.''

''I don't know. I mean, I don't know *yet*. I'm working on it.''

''Sounds like you got a lot of theory, but not a hell of a lot in the way of facts.'' Dejaye was a practical man and facts interested him more than speculation.

Pete felt a little flare of anger. ''I said I'm working on it. I just want to know if you had the equipment, it would be possible to make the jump.''

Dejaye fixed a hard look on Pete. "Buddy, to even think about jumping from a 747 you gotta be very skilled or very dick-brained. Which one do you want to talk to?"

Pete shook his head. "I don't get it. What do you mean?"

"Simple. Skill is a guy named Don Jagger. He's a world champion skydiver. Better than me. Better than just about everybody. . . ."

"And dick-brained?" Pete asked. "Who fits that description?"

Dejaye laughed. "Easy. Dick-brained is Jagger's old partner, Jess Crossman."

"And where would I find them?"

"Well . . ." Dejaye scratched his head. "I don't think they're jumping together anymore. But Jess Crossman lives real close to here. . . ."

7

The Sugarloaf Drop Zone occupied a few acres just off old Route A1, the main thoroughfare leading to the Florida Keys. It wasn't much to look at. All it consisted of was a few rundown old buildings, a concrete landing strip bordered by water on two sides, and what appeared to be a cemetery for old airplanes, an aviation junkyard full of dented, rusty fuselages, wings, props and flaps.

Pete parked his car, got out and looked around. Not far away a mechanic tinkered with the landing gear of a bruised and battered Piper Cub. Back near the hangar was a group of skydiving students, each dressed in brightly colored, form-fitting jumpsuits, tight nylon uniforms that hugged their bodies close. But they weren't doing anything more exciting than tossing bits of bread to a tame raccoon which lived in one of the old bits of airplane.

Directly in front of Pete was the oddest looking building on the field. It was a small hut up on stilts, a bunch of torn up Hawaiian shirts hanging in the open windows serving as colorful, if not very effective curtains. In front of the door was a sign: *Crossman Skydiving*.

This was the place.

Pete walked over to the mechanic. He was a young man with close-cropped blond hair and a wispy moustache. His overalls were so stained with oil and grease that Pete could only guess at the original color.

"Jess Crossman?" Pete asked.

The mechanic shook his head. "Not today."

"Know where I can find him?"

The mechanic hesitated for a moment, as if Pete had made some kind of faux pas and the young man was considering correcting him. He seemed to think better of it.

"Well, Jess should be here after a bit," was all he said. Then he turned back to the beat up under carriage of the old Piper.

"Think he'd mind if I waited inside?"

"Maybe," said the mechanic. "Don't know, really."

"Thanks," said Pete. He walked over to the door of the stilthouse and pushed open the canvas flap hanging in the doorway and stepped inside.

The place was a mess. There was a battered old gray metal office desk, almost buried under a profusion of paper—manuals, magazines, phone books and a very thick stack of bills and invoices, many marked "final demand" and "past due."

The newest piece of paper in the room was a fresh, red, white and blue flier advertising a Fourth of July Skydiving Exhibition and calling for experienced jumpers to take part.

The walls were covered with photographs. Staged group photographs of men and women in skydiving uniforms, along with candid pictures taken at jumps. Pete examined one picture closely, a photograph of a man holding aloft a huge loving cup. Watching him, laughing, was an attractive woman. He wore a cap that read: Team Jagger and scrawled across the bottom of the picture was a dedication: *"From the current world champ to the next.''* This, Pete assumed, was the famous, but elusive, Don Jagger. Without a moment of hesitation, Pete took the picture off the wall and pulled it out of the frame, sliding it into his pants pocket—it never hurt to have a photograph of a suspect.

If he'd had to choose, Pete would have been more interested in speaking to Jagger, the man Dejaye told him represented real skydiving skill. But Pete couldn't find him. So he had to settle for Jess Crossman, daredevil.

While he examined the photographs the sound of an airplane approaching gradually filled the air. It was droning up from the south, then circling the airfield. Pete stepped out onto the balcony of the stilt house to watch the airplane come in for a landing.

The plane was attempting to level off for a touchdown, but the wobble in the wings suggested that either the pilot was lousy or there was something seriously wrong with the aircraft. Pete could tell that he wasn't the only one worried about this bumpy landing. The skydiving students had forgotten about the raccoon and were watching as the plane touched down on the concrete runway.

The moment the aircraft was on the ground, the pilot threw the engines into reverse, slowed the craft down to a walk and brought it over to the front of the hangar. The engine died and a moment later the cockpit door swung open.

The pilot, a self-assured looking woman in her early thirties, walked under the balcony of the stilt house without giving Pete so much as a glance. As she passed the students she faked a smile.

''Pay no attention to the ragged landing, kids. Routine safety drill. Nothing to worry about . . .''

As she turned to face the mechanic her smile vanished.

She grabbed him by the lapel of his greasy overalls and marched him into the corner of the hangar.

"Selkirk! You should be fixing lawnmowers, not airplanes. I nearly got killed up there. Go check out the flaps, for God's sake."

"Sorry Winona," said Selkirk. "I'll get right on it. . . ." He turned to go, then stopped. "Listen, Winona, my new chute just arrived. Would you take me up later, just so I can try it out?"

"If you live that long," Winona grumbled.

"The next load is booked," someone said. Pete turned. The woman in the photographs with Jagger was standing in the doorway of the office. She did not look pleased to see him. "And this isn't a waiting room."

Jessie "Jess" Crossman, was a tall, lean woman in her twenties. There was a toughness in her voice that was real, not faked, a definite hint that she could take care of herself, come what may.

"Damn," said Pete. "I was dying to get on that plane."

Jessie looked him over, from his shoes to the top of his head. "So?" she said. "DEA? FBI? Or are you just one of our local police heroes?"

Pete was surprised. He knew that some cops just looked like cops—that no matter how far undercover they tried to go they would never look like anything but police officers trying to pass for normal members of society. Pete did not figure he fell into the category and was amazed that this woman had made him so quickly.

"I didn't think it was that obvious," he said. "Jess Crossman?"

"There are only two kinds of people who want to see me these days—skydivers and cops. And you don't look like any skydiver I've ever run into. Want a beer?"

Pete shook his head. "No."

His refusal didn't stop her from digging two cans of cold beer out of the small refrigerator in the corner of the office. She passed one to him.

"You know," she said, popping the tab on the can and taking a sip. "Cops I don't like—"

Pete nodded. "And let me guess why. Because every time you meet one was right after you'd broken the law. Am I right?"

Jess Crossman nodded. "Yeah." She put down her beer and looked Pete straight in the eye. "Okay. Let's get down to business. Did I go out of state last weekend without calling my parole officer? Yes. Guilty. I admit it. But it was an emergency. Okay?" She shook her head and looked disgusted. "Beats the hell out of me how you guys find these things out *and* why you give a damn. Seems to me the police have better things to do than worry about a parole violation."

"Parole violation?" said Pete.

"You're not here about a parole violation?"

Pete shook his head. "Nope."

Jess allowed herself a small smile but she didn't get any friendlier. In fact, she seemed more annoyed if anything. "But you *are* a cop?" she asked.

"Yes."

"Then why the hell are you here?"

"Did you hear about that 747 hijacking last week?"

Jessie nodded. "How could I miss it? What a major, first-class screwup, huh?"

"Suppose it wasn't a screwup," said Pete. "Suppose someone just wanted to make it look like one?"

"Then they did one hell of a job, I'd say." She swigged her beer. "But why would anyone want to do that?"

"Why?" said Pete. "To grab a prisoner. A prisoner I was escorting. They grab him . . . and jump." He made a little diving motion with his hand, as if it was all pretty straightforward.

Jessie considered this for a moment. "A jailbreak from a 747. That's a cool idea. No offense to you, but it is an inspired piece of thinking."

Pete realized that this pretty young woman was the first person who had not immediately poured cold water on his theory. He found himself feeling grateful to her for that small courtesy.

"Could you do it?" he asked.

"Am I a suspect?" Jessie countered.

"Why do you ask?"

Jessie smirked. "Lemme guess . . . 'Cause people told you that Jessie Crossman is the only person skilled enough to jump from a 747, right?"

Now it was Pete's opportunity to smirk. "Well . . . not quite. My source didn't talk about skill so much. The phrase used was dick-brained . . ."

"Some yahoo cop tried some John Wayne heroics on that 747 and a lot of people got killed—and *I'm* the dickbrain? Is that it?"

"That's not what happened," said Pete angrily. "And the yahoo cop was my brother."

Jessie drained her beer and shrugged. "Hey, sorry," she said, as if Pete's problems were trivial. "But if I'm not a suspect then I don't have to talk to you, do I?"

"You didn't answer my question about the jump," said Pete. "Could the jump be done?"

Jessie aimed the beer can at the trash bin and threw it, sinking it. "The longer I stand here, the broker I get," she said. "I've got students waiting, so you pay like

everyone else if you want to talk to me about jumping."
Then she turned on her heel and walked out of the room.

Pete hurried after her. "Look, all I want to know is
how a jump could be done. That's all you have to tell
me—"

"Pay me."

"How much?"

"Lessons are fifty bucks a throw. Rental of equipment
is fifty a day. Fifty plus fifty," she said. "You do the
math, officer."

"A hundred bucks and you'll tell me what I want to
know, right?"

"Let's see the money . . ."

Pete sighed and shook his head. He pulled out his bill-
fold and flipped it open. "Here. Five twenties. That cover
it?"

Jessie shoved him into the room adjoining the office.
It was stuffed with skydiving gear. She threw a bulky
nylon jump suit and tandem harness at him.

"Put that on," Jessie ordered.

Pete frowned. "What do I need this get up for if we're
just going to talk?"

"My drop zone," said Jessie. "My rules." She flashed
him a sly little smile. "Say, you're not scared, are you?"

Pete felt like a jerk. He came out of the office dressed in
his jumpsuit—a fetching, snug body sheath consisting of
bright pink spandex pants with yellow piping and a sky
blue top with tight sleeves edged in the same pink as his
trousers. He was sure that Jessie had chosen the most
embarrassing set on purpose, just to put him on his
guard—as if he wasn't already.

Winona's plane was on the runway, the twin engines
roaring, the propellers slashing the humid morning air.

The four students were in place, Jessie at the door. As Pete climbed in, Selkirk, the mechanic came running up to the plane, carrying his new parachute rig.

"Hey, Jess," he shouted over the sound of the props. "I was wondering—"

Jess Crossman shook her head. "Uh-uh, Selkirk. Some other time."

The young man's face fell, but he dropped back. Pete had no doubts about who was boss around here. *My drop zone,* Jessie had said, *my rules* . . . And she meant it.

Winona took the plane up to fifteen thousand feet, the door open all the way. Pete forced himself to look out and down. The view was scary. He had never considered himself a nervous flier, in fact, he had never given air travel a moment of thought—it was just a fact of modern life. You got on a plane, you ate the lousy food, you watched the movie and then you got off—and hoped your luggage made it.

This was different. The plane seemed flimsy, rocking and bucking in the air currents, the engines beating like puny fists against the great forces of the wind and sky. Pete felt uncomfortable, sick in the pit of his stomach, afraid of the vast space around him—but there was another fear he had to contend with, one he hadn't expected: he was also terrified of looking bad.

Jessie Crossman, by contrast, was right at home. She seemed at ease in her black bodysuit and parachute rig. It was obvious that she was in her element here, adrenaline pumping her up like a drug.

Her students huddled about her. "Give me a controlled exit and good arch," she yelled. "Let that air sculpt your body position. Got it?"

They nodded and gave her thumbs up.

"Go!" Jessie ordered.

As if they were doing nothing more dangerous than stepping off a curb on a quiet street, the four students fell out of the airplane, peeling out into the slip stream and zooming away in the air.

Pete watched them go with a shake of his head. "I don't see the attraction," he yelled in Jessie's ear.

"Haven't you ever watched a bird gliding on the wind?" she asked. "And haven't you ever wished you could do the same thing?"

Pete nodded. "Sure. For about thirty seconds."

"You just don't get it, do you?"

"Sure I get it," he said. "I'm just wondering how much skill it takes to jump out of an airplane, count to twenty and pull a damn string?"

Jessie pointed out the open door at the students who were getting smaller and smaller as they free-fell. Their arms and legs were wide apart.

"See the wind force their bodies open?" said Jessie. "We're only at eighty knots."

"Yeah? So?"

"A 747 travelling at five hundred knots could rip a jumper clean apart. That's where the skill comes in."

"It's no big deal," said Pete dismissively.

Jessie threw Pete a scary smile. "You know, you're out of your league up here, cowboy."

"Yeah?" he shouted. "I keep hearing about skill, but if you're so damn good, what are you doing working in this shithole drop zone?"

Jessie's eyes glittered. "If *you're* so damn good, how come you've got a dead brother?"

It was a low blow and in that instant Pete hated this cocky, self-confident young woman. "I'm paying you for this shit?"

"Yeah."

62

"So make it worth my while."

"Okay." Jessie pulled a level at the base of the plane fuselage. The old bomb bay doors beneath Pete's feet popped open and in a split second he dropped, without a parachute, out of the plane. He was so surprised, he couldn't even manage a scream.

Winona turned in the pilot's seat. "Very funny, Jess. Now go and get him."

Jessie shrugged. "He paid for one jump . . . might as well give him one."

"Okay," shouted Winona. "You've made your point. For Christ sake, just go and get him, okay?"

"All right, all right," as if she was a teenager being told to take out the trash. "I'm going."

Jessie dove into the air, making her body as small as possible, presenting as small a lift surface as possible, knifing through the air. In a matter of seconds she was travelling at two hundred miles per hour, speeding like an air to air missile locked on her target—the flailing body of Pete a few hundred feet below her.

Peter couldn't even think of the words of a prayer. He was screaming into the wind, an inchoate mass of panicky sounds, that could hardly be heard over the rushing of the wind. His face was distorted by wind, the force of gravity and the deep terror that gripped him. It was the ultimate nightmare—rocketing toward earth with no chute, no wings, no chance. It was all over.

Winona had put the plane into a dive, tracking Pete and Jessie, dropping down fast to witness the rescue. She knew Jessie was good, of course, but in a situation like this there were no guarantees.

It took five seconds for Jessie to catch up with Pete, but she was travelling so fast that it looked as if she would flash right by him. At the very last moment, Jessie pivoted in the sky, seemingly stopping dead in the sky—in actual fact, she had managed to slow herself down to his speed. Then she did a half front flap and caught Pete between her knees in a leg scissors catch. Quickly, she connected the quick snap to his tandem harness and pulled open her chute.

There was a blinding flash of bright red fabric followed by the loud *whump!* as the wind caught the cloth. Pete felt himself yanked up into the air, as if caught in an undertow. Then things seemed to calm down, the currents felt less strong, the air less angry.

He felt calm enough to get mad at her. "You are totally crazy!" he yelled at Jessie. "Completely out of your goddamned mind!"

"Yeah," she yelled back. "Maybe."

They landed on the edge of the Sugarloaf Drop Zone, skirting the field and touching down in the gentle lap of surf on the shore of the pond. The touch down was as light as a feather.

Jessie unhooked the tandem and started hauling in her parachute. "Welcome to the sky," she said matter of factly, as if people fell out of airplanes every day of the week. "I thought you did okay."

"You did, huh?" It was all Pete could do to contain his volcanic anger.

Jessie nodded. "Yeah. You fell. You lived. Good start."

"I see." Then he punched her as hard as he could in the face, knocking her into the shallow water. She rolled once and looked up. She was holding her cheek, her mouth open, feeling more amazement than pain.

"What the hell was that?"

"You fell. You lived. Goodbye."

• • •

Pete went back to the office, peeled off his jumpsuit and then walked to his car. He felt bruised and beaten up, as if he had been in a fight. His nerves were jangled, his hair a mess, and as the adrenaline began to wear off he felt bone tired—a reaction, a defense mechanism against the delayed shock of his near miss with a horrifying death.

Winona had landed the plane and she and Selkirk fell in step with him.

"Hey," she said.

Pete said nothing, he just kept on walking eyes down, looking neither left nor right.

Winona refused to give up. "Hey, I didn't know she was going to do that."

"It was probably safer than landing in that damn death trap you call a plane."

Winona smiled. "Well . . . not quite."

Pete stopped and faced them both. "You want to help? Tell me where I can find Don Jagger. Any ideas?"

"There's a big jump this weekend in Ocean Reef," said Selkirk. "All the hot ones will be there. That's probably your best bet."

"Thanks." Pete dug his car keys out of his pocket. "I appreciate it."

Winona shot an angry look at Selkirk. "You know, skydivers are a pretty tight group. You'll have a tough time breaking through all by yourself."

"I'll take my chances," said Pete curtly. "Thanks."

Winona shrugged. "Whatever."

"Don't hold it against Jessie," said Selkirk. "Ever since Jagger went south on her she's been kind of touchy." He tried to make it sound as if dropping a defenseless stranger out of an airplane was a perfectly natural response to a love affair gone sour. Maybe in the world of skydiving it was.

"What happened to Jagger?" Pete asked.

"Everybody says he got suckered into making a few drug jumps," Selkirk explained. "He did time for it. So did Jessie. They haven't patched things up since."

Winona was protective of Jessie and she glared at Selkirk, silently urging him to shut up. But he didn't get the hint.

"Does she want to patch things up?" said Pete. "If someone fixed it so you got time in the joint, would you?"

"Well," said Selkirk. "She's loyal. I'll give her that." He turned to Winona. "You know her better than anyone. What do you think?"

"I think it's time for you to zip it and go fix the rear whammer-jammy on the tail," she said.

Selkirk shrugged and looked at Pete as he got into his car. "By the way—that was a good first jump."

Pete half smiled. "And it wasn't a bad *last* jump either."

8

The Twin Otter circled Ty Moncrief's swamp base, jigged once to the left, and then rose. The plane was being flown by the team's wheelman, a small, feral-faced man named Deuce—he had a sure hand with any kind of vehicle, on the ground or in the air. And his veins seemed to be filled with some kind of coolant, rather than blood—he would put a plane into tighter corners than any pilot should dare.

As the Twin Otter sailed higher into the clear sky, Don Jagger dropped out of the plane, a howling, terrified Leedy yoked to his tandem. It was a simple, straightforward piggyback jump, but to hear Leedy, screaming all the way down, you would have thought they were free-falling into hell itself.

The instant they hit, Jagger cut away his chute, unhooked Leedy then rushed him across the mushy terrain into the house. The rest of the team was waiting there, cheering them on, Ty Moncrief standing by with a stopwatch.

Jagger pushed Leedy toward a stack of gleaming computer equipment. "There it is, Leedy. Go for it." Then he turned to Moncrief. "How did we do on time?"

Moncrief clicked the stopwatch and nodded. "Good. You did good. Made it with time to spare."

"Would have been faster if Leedy would cooperate more," said Jagger.

"Yes," said Moncrief with a mildness that every person in the room found a little chilling. "That would be nice, wouldn't it."

Leedy was slumped in front of the computer keyboard, trembling as if the air in the muggy room was subzero.

"Do your job, Leedy," said Moncrief.

Leedy raised his tear-stained face. "I can't. I'm too upset to even think."

"I said, do your job." Moncrief's tone of voice was far from mild now."

"Please . . . I need a minute to steady myself. Please, let me just—ack!"

Ty Moncrief had pounced on him like a bird of prey, grabbing him by the throat and hauling him out of the chair. "When we're in, you're going to have seconds, not minutes, Leedy. You've got to work *fast*. Understand?"

"But . . . but after a jump my nerves are shot. I just can't think straight. I'm sorry."

Ty shoved the hapless Leedy into Don Jagger's arms. "Jump him till he can think straight."

"Maybe he's had enough for one day," said Jagger wearily.

"But I haven't," Ty snapped. He fixed an icy stare on Jagger. "Get him out of here."

Jagger nodded and grabbed Leedy, who whimpered pathetically, pulling him out of the room. The rest of the crew followed, knowing instinctively that the boss was in no mood for company.

Ty sat himself down in the seat that Leedy had just vacated. He pressed a few buttons on the keyboard, entering a series of commands. In a matter of seconds a large box appeared on the screen, moving vertically, rising up, lines shooting through it until it formed the schematics of an office building.

Moncrief rested his chin in his hand and studied the plan, deep in thought, as if trying to work out a fiendishly complicated problem on a three-dimensional chess board.

Over the years, the United States Marshal's Service had placed Pete Nessip in a number of sticky situations. But that morning he had the uneasy feeling that all the unpleasant predicaments of the past would pale before the one he faced that day. Interrogating children who had been witnesses to violent crime was always a difficult, delicate thing to do.

He parked his car at the curb in a quiet suburban street and picked up a big, fluffy toy—a stuffed tiger—on the seat next to him. He hoped that it was at least *close* to being like the one Lena had lost on the plane, but he had no detailed recollections at all of what the thing had looked like. Big, brown eyes, soft—that was about it.

He had spoken to Lena's mother, Alice Willens, earlier that morning, identifying himself as a US Marshal but not mentioning that he was suspended from the service pending the findings of a board of review. Alice Willens just assumed that he was the latest in the long line of law enforcement and other government officials who had come by to talk to her little daughter.

As he walked up the flagstone path to the house, a dun-colored Dodge sedan pulled up to the curb, parking behind his own car. There were two men in the car, but neither of them got out. They just sat, watching the Willen house.

"Miami police," Mrs. Willen explained. "They watch the house for a couple of hours every day and they come

69

by at night too. They've been very kind. I think it makes Lena feel a little more secure to have them here.''

''How is she?'' Pete asked.

''Physically she's fine. I think she's still a little puzzled by what happened. She has forgotten just about all of it which the doctor says is a perfectly normal defense mechanism. In time, she won't remember it happened at all. . . .''

As she spoke, she led Pete through the house and into the small, tidy backyard. Lena had just gotten home from school—her little backpack was open on the table—and she was playing on the patio but seemed unsurprised to see Pete. Not that she remembered him from the flight, but because she was getting used to all kinds of policemen coming to see her to ask her questions.

''Hey, Lena,'' said Pete. ''This is for you!'' He held out the tiger.

''Wow!'' The little girl took the stuffed toy with obvious delight, throwing her arms around the soft, furry neck of the tiger. ''Thank you!''

Pete crouched down, until he was face-to-face with the little girl. ''Lena,'' he said quietly, ''your mother said I could ask you some questions about your plane trip. Would that be okay with you?''

With that intense solemnity that children display on occasion, Lena nodded gravely. ''Uh-huh.''

''The FBI showed her some photographs of terrorists,'' said Mrs. Willens. ''I'm afraid Lena didn't recognize any.''

''That's okay,'' said Pete, pulling up a cast-iron patio chair. He looked Lena in the eye. ''When you got on the plane, Lena, do you remember who you sat next to? Was it a man or a woman.''

''I . . . I don't remember,'' she said. ''I'm sorry—''

"That's okay, that's okay," said Pete soothingly. He took a snapshot of his brother from the inside pocket of his suit jacket. "Do you remember this man?"

Lena took the picture in her hands and studied it closely for a moment. She shook her head. "No."

"Okay." Pete put a hand on his chest. "What about me? Do you remember me? Remember how your tiger bumped me on the head when you got on the plane?"

Very slowly, Lena shook her head from side to side, an emphatic no.

"Do you remember hearing anything during the flight?" he asked gently. "A loud noise, maybe?"

"No," she said firmly. "I fell asleep and when I woke up we were landed."

Pete felt the tiniest pinprick of frustration. The little girl had been so traumatized by what had taken place that she had buried the evil memories deep down.

From inside the house, they could hear the phone ringing. The mother looked at her little girl and then at Pete, as if struggling with herself, unsure of leaving her alone. One side of the internal argument prevailed. "I'll just go—" said Mrs. Willens, rising and running to the phone.

Pete waited a moment, then he took out another picture. This one was a shot of the damaged 747 lying on the ground at the crash site.

"Lena . . . this is the plane you took," he whispered, laying the photograph on the table in front of her. "Do you remember?"

The little girl stared at the ugly picture, the slightest flicker of recognition flitting across her features.

"There was smoke," said Pete. "Yelling. Then there was a big explosion. . . ." He placed another picture on the table. This one showed the interior of the aircraft, the torn-up rear section of the plane where he and Terry and Lena had sat. She gazed at it for a moment, then he laid another one over that, a grotesque picture of the site of the explosion itself—a study in melted plastic and twisted, charred metal.

"This is where the big explosion happened," he said. "Remember? There was a wind, a big wind. . . ."

The little girl stared at the picture for a long time. Pete could see that he was getting through to her, that there was some glimmer of recollection in her mind. Her brow darkened as old memories began to stir.

"A . . . a big noise?" said Lena.

"That's right." He tapped the picture of the blown-away door. "It blew a great big hole in the back of the plane," he whispered.

As Pete spoke, his voice seemed to become indistinct and Lena found herself lost in her memories. Under his prompting, it was coming back to her now—the chaos, the noise, the smoke. She could see it clearly.

"The wind was howling," said Pete. "It sucked things back toward the hole . . ."

Lena could see the drinks cart hurtling down the aisle toward the maw. She could hear screams. The little girl stroked the soft fur of her tiger, caressing it as if it was a lucky charm that would ward off evil.

"You saw someone . . ."

Lena remembered that she was pulled from her seat, yanked down the passageway by the force of the sucking wind. She remembered grabbing on to a man, she remembered grabbing something he wore on his back.

The little girl pointed to her school backpack. "He wore one of those," she whispered.

Pete nodded, doing his best to contain his excitement. "That's right. Like a backpack. I saw that too."

Lena was telling him exactly what he wanted to hear—and he could tell from the intense, serious look on her face that this was the unvarnished gospel truth.

Lena didn't need any prompting now. She could see herself clearly, as if watching a movie. She could see herself grabbing at Jagger's clothes, desperately trying to hold on, fighting the wind which was going to pull her from the airplane. She did not know what was beyond that door, but she did not want to go there. She remembered her hands closing around the oxygen mask the man wore and pulling it away from his face. She remembered the scar beneath his eye. . . .

"His face," she whispered. "He had . . ."

Pete was leaning forward, his forehead almost touching Lena's. "He had what, Lena? Tell me."

"Oh my God," said Mrs. Willens. "What is going on? What are you doing?"

"We're remembering." Pete did not look up. He kept his eyes focused on the little girl. Lena was trembling now, clutching the tiger around its soft neck.

Mrs. Willens grabbed her little girl and enfolded her in a protective hug. "Get out of my house! Right now!"

"Please," pleaded Pete.

"Get out now! Or I'm calling the police."

"I was almost—"

Mrs. Willens started around the side of the house making for the police car that was still parked in the street. "Officer!" the woman called. "Please . . ."

Pete knew he had only seconds left. "Lena, what else? I know you saw something else. What about his face. . . . Tell me about his face."

She remembered. She looked into Pete's own face, her eyes fastening on the half moon shaped scar under his eye. Pete touched the ridge of tissue. "One of these? He had a scar like this?"

Lena nodded. Pete held up the picture he had stolen from Jessie's office. "Is this the man?"

The little girl looked at the picture and her eyes grew wide. Her mouth dropped open—and Pete could almost feel her fear. He hated himself for badgering her, but he had to know.

"Is this the man?"

Lena could not answer him—not in words, anyway. But the look on her face told him that she recognized the face of Don Jagger.

Then he felt a heavy hand on his shoulder. "Okay," said one of the cops. "That's enough."

In a matter of minutes, police from all over Dade county converged on that quiet suburban street. A couple of uniforms came first, followed by a car full of detectives, among them Norm Fox, the Miami cop who had checked out the plane with Pete.

Last to arrive was McCracken. And he looked far from happy at the circumstances of the call.

"Okay," said Pete as soon as he saw his boss. He knew he was going to have to talk fast. "The girl gave up one of the hijackers." He showed the picture of Jagger. "This man. He's—"

"I don't give a damn!" McCracken hustled Pete across the lawn to the curb.

"But Tom, she saw a parachute on his back and he has a scar under his eye that—"

"Shuttup, Pete. Just shut up." The other detectives were standing around, listening to him chew out his agent. "Are you out of your mind?"

"If you'd just listen."

But McCracken was angry enough to hit Pete. "No. You listen. Do you honestly believe that a crazed, suspended US Marshal badgering a traumatized ten-year-old into remembering a parachute and a scar amounts to evidence? Are you nuts or what?"

"I saw it," said Pete stubbornly. "I saw it in her eyes. She knew him."

McCracken shook his head. "Listen to yourself, Pete. The kid would have ID'd Donald Duck just to get you to stop. You really crossed the line this time."

"But—"

"No buts. Let me spell this out for you. You get your face dirty again on this absurd chase, and there is nothing I can do for you. Got it?"

"You should believe me, Tom," said Pete slowly. "I know I have something here."

McCracken was angry but deep down he was sad too. His best agent was cracking up right in front of his eyes and there was nothing he could do to stop it. "I wish I could, Pete. I wish I could. But no, I don't believe you."

"It's the truth."

"Take a trip, Pete. Do yourself a favor and get out of town. Way out of town. But let it go. Please. It's for your own good."

Pete did not know it, but there was one man on the scene that morning who believed him. Detective Fox overheard the brief, angry exchange between the two marshals and knew that someone would be interested in what Pete had to say.

The cop wandered away from the knot of policemen. Once out of earshot, he took a cellular phone from his pocket, flipped it open and punched in a number quickly.

"Yes," he said. "Special Agent Talmidge please . . . Talmidge? This is Detective Fox of the Miami PD?"

On the other end of the line, Ty Moncrief smiled. "Why Detective Fox," he said. "How nice to hear from you." The money he had paid Fox had been well spent.

Fox continued to pretend that he was talking to the FBI—just in case someone could hear him. "Yes . . . Concerning the airplane accident you were investigating. The other US Marshal on the plane seems to have acquired some information I thought I should pass on to you. . . ."

"The other marshal?" said Moncrief.

"That's correct. The young lady on the plane gave him a partial ID of one of the hijackers. She said something about a scar under his left eye."

Ty considered this bit of information for a moment. "Well, thank you," he said. "I'm very impressed."

"Thank you," said Fox. He figured that he had proven his worth—and that there was probably another fifteen or twenty thousand coming his way.

But Moncrief cut him down to size in a matter of seconds. "Not with you," he said curtly. "With this marshal." Ty hung up and thought for a moment. The marshal was making a nuisance of himself and would have to be taken care of at some point—but first things first.

It was the third jump of the day for Moncrief's team, another routine training drop from the Otter over the target that had been marked in the swamp. Deuce, at the controls, was as bored as a bus driver.

Ty went first, bailing out of the plane early, slowing his descent so he could watch the rest of his crew fall past him, evaluating their performance like a strict teacher.

Torski was next out, dropping toward the ground with Leedy hooked up to the tandem. Moncrief could just make out his screams as they rocketed by. Leedy would never

76

get used to skydiving—the best Moncrief could hope for was that he could settle his nerves fast enough to be of use. Without the computer nerd the whole operation was useless—still, Ty was looking forward to the time when he would no longer require the assistance of the annoying little fellow.

Jagger and Kara came next. In contrast to Leedy, these two revelled in the open air. They went out of the plane without a moment of hesitation and played in the rushing air like kids frolicking in a warm surf.

In perfect order the three chutes below Moncrief popped open like big black mushrooms against the blue sky. The team worked their toggles to align their approach, all three of them on line for the target.

Moncrief delayed a moment, getting closer to Jagger before deploying his own chute. He bore down from above and top docked him, sliding his feet into Jagger's steering lines, plucking him out of the sky, like an eagle snatching up prey with his talons. From that moment on, Jagger could only go where Moncrief chose to take him.

At first, Jagger thought this was just another bit of Ty Moncrief's bullshit, macho posturing, another lesson in showing his team who was the boss.

Ty overshot the drop zone, carrying Jagger away to the east. Below them Torski and Kara hit the ground, wrapped up their chutes and watched as the two men soared by them.

On the horizon was a strand of high voltage power lines strung between two pylons. Ty looked down and saw that Jagger was looking up at him. He was pointing and shouting, but his voice was lost to the wind.

There was terror on Jagger's face now and he rocked in his harness, fighting for control of his rig, but Moncrief had him locked down, trapped in the web. The power lines were only a hundred yards away now and they were closing in fast.

When they hit, Jagger's agonized screams were loud enough to reach up into the air. Ty dumped him into the thicket of high tension wires, then flew over him and dropped for the ground, watching as Jagger's body sparked and burnt on the lines. In a matter of seconds the electricity surged through his body, stopping his heart mid-beat. His lifeless body hung suspended for a moment, the crackle of sparks burning through his jumpsuit, branding his flesh. Then he crashed through the lines and his corpse fell to the ground with a sickening thud. The air was filled with the smell of burning meat.

Ty hit the ground and scrambled, walking quickly to the remaining members of his team. Torski, Kara, and Leedy stared at him, tensed and ready to run—there were three of them and only one of him, but Ty Moncrief scared them all to death.

"You signed on for the ride of your lives and money forever," said Moncrief looking from face to face. "Jagger became a liability. We go in with five. Any problems?"

Each one of them shook their heads. If they did entertain any doubts, they knew they were in too deep to do anything about them. The only way out of the operation at this late date was to follow the deadly trail blazed by Jagger.

9

Selkirk said that all of the hot jumpers in South Florida would be in Ocean Reef that weekend, but Pete was unprepared for how large an event this would be. Once over Seven Mile Bridge, the main bridge connecting the Florida Keys with the mainland, he hit a steady stream of cars, all of them heading for the meet. When he got to the little town, he found it was packed with people, the main street clogged with traffic.

He drove straight through town to the drop zone. It was much more elaborate than Jessie Crossman's threadbare operation. This one was stretched over a dozen acres and was made up of four separate runways, all overseen from a tall control tower, plus a series of hangars and workshops. In the middle of the complex was the huge landing area for the skydivers, the gravel filled targets marked with circles of whitewash.

All of the competition, landing and hangar areas were secure behind cyclone fencing and there was a security post at the gate. The guard flagged Pete down as he tried to drive through.

"Your pass is supposed to be in the windshield, mister," said the guard. "Not in your pocket."

"I'm looking for a buddy," said Pete. "He's a skydiver."

"Ain't they all." The guard did not look like a happy man. Skydivers were an unruly crowd, a bunch of rowdy young men and women who thought that the only rule that applied to them was the law of gravity—and they enjoyed flouting that convention as well.

"So if I could just drive on to the property and see if he's there—"

The security guard shook his head. "Can't let you without a pass. Besides, it wouldn't do any good—there's nobody there. Why don't you look down at Alabama Jacks? It's a bar they all hang out at."

"Thanks. Where is it?"

"On the water," said the guard. "You can't miss it."

He was right. Alabama Jacks was a shack, a funky shack hanging over the water, open on all sides. The patrons seemed to be divided pretty equally between the skydivers and fishermen—the boats mooring at a jetty just beyond the front door.

The place was packed and the air was full of music, thumping so loud the worn floorboards seemed to vibrate with the heavy bass beat. The drinkers ranged in age from the kids who had turned twenty-one that day and had the ID to prove it, all the way up to men and women in their mid-sixties. There was a range of clothing styles too—everything from jumpers in high tech spandex speed bodysuits to guys in torn jeans and painters overalls. Pete noticed that there was one thing all the skydivers seem to have in common—whether they were dressed in sharp, high tech gear or in torn jeans and ripped T-shirts—to a man they were slobs. No one seemed to shave—from ZZ Top style beards to just a few days stubble, no one was clean shaven. No one seemed to wash or even comb their hair either.

Some of the big time professionals wore the logos of

their high profile corporate sponsors—beer companies, fast food chains and the makers of expensive sneakers— and they strutted around the bar with all the self-confidence that goes with being at the top of your sport.

Although the place was packed and patrons were standing three deep at the bar, Pete noticed a couple of tables were empty, no one going near them as if they stood on hallowed ground. He cruised the room for a minute or two, listening to the buzz. Over the music, he could hear the constant jabber of non-stop war stories and the shop talk.

". . . hell, you ever jump those round chutes?"

"Hell yes! Couldn't steer the damn things and never knew where you'd land. . . . I've got enough branches up my ass to start a forest fire. . . ."

". . . testing the prototype reserve chutes. . . ."

"Opened up at five grand like a good boy should, but the next thing you know the thing folds up like a wet Kleenex. . . ."

". . . whole bunch of DZs that don't accept non-TSOed gear. Right? Am I right or what?"

". . . now I'm gonna burn in, but then I see a big white tent on lawn a mile away, so what the hell, I track for it. . . ."

". . . Airport is five hundred yards on the left, see, next to the nude beach for high school cheerleaders. . . ."

"I hammer in and when I come to I'm surrounded by people dressed in white. I'm sure I'm dead, but it turns out I landed in a wedding. Knocked the bride out stone cold. . . ."

". . . somebody lightbulbs the idea to base jump the Arco Tower at three in the morning. We landed on top of a security guard. The good news is he was more stoned than we were. . . ."

Pete waved at a waitress, trying to get her attention, but she ignored him, breezing right by him as if he wasn't there. She stopped next to him, waiting on three guys in jumpsuits.

"So what are we all drinking today?" she asked, flashing the three jumpers a bright smile.

"Three Buds."

"Got it."

"Bitch," Pete muttered under his breath. He settled at one of the empty seats, then swivelled around and looked over the bar. There were three TV sets suspended above the bar—in another joint they would have been tuned to whatever sport was being played that season, but in Alabama Jacks they played videos of that day's jumps. Between the TV sets hung a big brass ship's bell.

Four guys, each dressed in identical green competition gear, strode into the bar and walked over to Pete's table. Three of them dropped into the three vacant chairs, the fourth, the green leader stood over Pete, eyeballing him.

"Is this your table?" said Pete. "Sorry, I didn't know. Let me buy you a beer."

The green leader smiled a big phony smile. "Sure."

Pete pulled a twenty dollar bill out of his wallet and beckoned to the waitress, but before he could get her attention, the guy in green yanked him out of the chair and snatched the twenty out of his hand. Then he spun him away, into the arms of another member of the team—but before he could be passed on to the next guy, Pete swung and smacked one of the divers in the face. A nice solid, satisfying backhand. The man folded and went down.

Pete cocked his fists, ready to take on the whole bar if necessary. These guys were beginning to get on his nerves—big time. Then a firm hand grabbed his fist.

"I see you've met some skydivers," said Jessie.

"He with you, Jess?" asked the Green Team leader.

"Yeah. He's with me."

"Then I guess we'll have to beat the crap out of him when you aren't here."

"Some other time, ace," said Pete. He snatched back his twenty and handed it to the waitress. "Get them each a beer." He pointed to the guy still sprawled on the floor. "And a pillow for him."

Jessie hustled him away to her corner of the bar. Winona sat on a bar stool watching the action.

"Big deal. So these guys jump out of airplanes?" said Pete angrily. "How does that qualify them for this big fuckin' attitude?"

"You're not much of a cop, but you make friends easily, don't you?" said Jessie.

Pete grimaced and lowered his voice. "If you blow my cover you can kiss your paroled ass good-bye."

Jessie laughed. "Looks like you're doing a pretty good job of blowing your own cover," she said. "Come on, sit down. Let me buy you a beer."

"No, thanks."

"Listen, jack," said Jessie. "At the moment we're the only cover you've got." She patted the seat of the bar stool. "Have a seat."

Pete had the distinct feeling that Jessie was working some kind of angle. This sudden burst of cooperation intrigued him—considering that the last time they met she took a pretty good shot at killing him.

"Look," he said, "all I want is a little talk with your old friend Jagger. Give me that and you'll never see me again. That's a promise."

"Then here's what I want," Jessie countered, her voice low and urgent. "There's a big exhibition jump up in DC next week. I want to go, but my parole officer won't let me travel out of state."

"Yeah. Keep talking." The bartender slapped down three long-necked bottles of Budweiser. Pete picked his up and took a deep gulp.

"You've got a problem," she said, all business now. "The only way you'll ever learn anything is to hang with the best jumpers. But around here you stick out like a cub scout in a whorehouse."

Pete nodded, catching her drift immediately. "So if I grease your parole officer so you can do this DC jump, then you'll work me in with these guys? Is that it?"

"Smart boy," said Jessie nodding. "What do you say? We have a deal?"

But before he could answer, the bartender reached and clanged the bell once. Instantly, the bar went quiet as all conversation ceased.

"Burn in!" he shouted. "Drinks up!"

Every person in the bar hoisted a bottle or glass.

"Blue skies!" the bartender bellowed.

"Black death!" shouted the crowd.

Then they all knocked back their drinks in a single gulp. Pete looked around, puzzled by this sudden show of unity.

"What the hell is this?" he asked.

"It means a skydiver burned in somewhere today," Winona explained.

"Burned in?"

"As in crash landed . . . dead. They'll ring the bell and raise a toast every hour 'till midnight."

"Great tradition," he said, deadpan. "I know that would make *me* feel a lot better."

There was a real buzz going through the bar now, people were talking low as the name of the unfortunate jumper went from table to table.

"So who hammered in?" asked Winona.

"Don Jagger," said the bartender. "Cops found him with a load of cocaine . . . got tangled up in power lines. Dumb bastard."

All the color had drained from Jessie's face and her mouth dropped open. "Power lines?" she gasped. "You're telling me that he floated into power lines?"

"That's what I heard," said the bartender.

Winona threw an arm around her friend, trying to comfort her. She knew how much Don Jagger had meant to her—even if he had been nothing but trouble from the gitgo.

Jessie shook her head. "No. There's no way. Jagger was the best. There's no way he'd make a bullshit first timer mistake with power lines. Impossible."

Winona started to lead her toward the door. "Come on, Jess, let's get out of here."

"Hey," said Pete. "I'm sorry but . . ."

Jessie stopped, her back to him. She thought for a moment—Jagger had been murdered. She was sure of it and she was going to do something about it. She whirled around and got right in his face. "If you want my help—you've got it. All you have to do is pay for me and my airplane."

"How much?"

"Fifteen thousand," she said without hesitating for an instant.

"Fifteen thousand! Bullshit!"

"That's the number, jack," she said. "Besides, what do you care? It's the government's money."

"It's *my* case," he said. "Not the governments."

"Then I guess I'll be seeing you later." Jessie broke

free from Winona and stalked out of the bar, walking all the way out to the end of the jetty. She was facing the wide open sea, under the curved dome of the evening sky. In a second, the tears started. . . .

10

The airplane streaked through the night sky, low and fast, navigational lights off. It was a moving dark spot on the dark sky, almost invisible above the bright lights of downtown Miami. At the door, Ty Moncrief was bent over the glowing green screen of the miniature Loran screen strapped to his chest, studying the ever-changing diagram of the city-scape a few thousand feet below.

The rest of the team—Kara, Deputy Dog and Leedy locked to Torski's tandem—stood by, ready to jump. Beneath their jump suits each one of them was dressed in a dark blue uniform—the uniform of the Miami police department.

"Now," said Ty, signalling out the door.

At his gesture, each member of the team peeled off and fell into the night. The four black parachutes popped open, floating like small storm clouds over the sprawling urban landscape below. They stacked quickly, with Ty on top, using his Loran to navigate, tracking through the canyons of office towers.

The roof of the Miami Police Department headquarters was dotted with communication antenna, hump-backed air conditioning units and the shallow dishes of microwave satellite transponders. Each skydiver in the team had a pre-arranged landing spot, an open point in among all the equipment, and as they neared the roof they peeled out of the stack and hit their targets.

There was no wasted motion. The entire crew was rehearsed and ready, piling their chutes away from the wind, ready for a quick getaway. They were almost completely silent . . .

Deputy Dog and Kara rapidly swept the roof for alarms, finding two sensors. Torski slipped thimble-like metal probes onto his index fingers, then placed a hard plastic mouthpiece between his teeth, nodding at Kara, showing that he was ready for the juice.

Kara tapped fine wires into the wall sensors, signalling to Torski when she was finished. He jammed his fingers into the sensors, just as she activated the power pack strapped to her chest. The current connected through Torski, his body arching in pain, his face contorted with the rush of power.

Then he pulled his fingers back leaving the thimbles in place, jamming the security signal. He stepped back and spat out the mouthpiece—he had nearly bitten clean through it.

Moncrief popped open the door and led his team through the door, the four of them silently dashing down the metal steps into the guts of the silent building.

The first few floors of the Miami Police Department headquarters were busy twenty-four hours out of every twenty-four. It was here that cops checked in and out before their shifts and those floors also contained the interrogation rooms, the lock-up and the drunk tanks, the booking sergeant and the night court.

The upper floors were only open for business from nine to five—there was nothing up there but offices for the brass and some of the district attorneys as well as the laboratories and evidence room.

There was a police officer stationed at the reception desk on the fourth floor providing security—it was considered pretty soft duty by the cops in the station. How much security did a police facility need—who was going to break into a police station?

The bored cop was noshing on a sandwich and watching TV—*Jeopardy!* was his favorite show—all the while oblivious to the silent movements around him.

The category was sports legends which the cop figured he would be pretty good at.

Alex Trebek asked the question. "Only NBA hall-of-famer to play and coach his team to a world title in the same season."

On the screen the contestants appeared perplexed by the question—you didn't get a lot of rabid sports fans appearing on *Jeopardy!*—but the cop knew the answer.

"Russell," he said through a mouthful of liverwurst. "Bill Russell."

"Sorry," said a voice behind him. "It must be in the form of a question—*who* is Bill Russell?"

The cop turned and saw Ty Moncrief coming at him with a knife—it was the last thing he saw. In a split second the blue steel of the knife sliced deep into his throat and he fell to the floor, his life pumping out of him in a bright red stream.

With security taken care of, the team went to work. Leedy made his way to the computer room, a facility locked with an electronic security device wired into a combination lock. Leedy slipped what looked like a credit card into the slot of the electronic lock and wired the card to the random sequencer which he pulled from the equipment sack on his back. Quickly he patched the sequencer into his laptop and turned it on—in a matter of seconds thousands of numbers began to scroll across the screen.

Kara went for the evidence room. The patrolman on duty there opened the receiving window expecting to get some evidence to log in. Instead he got a faceful of pistol—his eyes went wide when he saw the fat silencer screwed to the business end of the Heckler and Koch. They closed tight when she shot him twice through the heart.

Then it was Torski's turn. He moved up with a pair of heavy-duty bolt cutters, cutting through the flimsy lock of the cage door. He and Kara darted into the darkened room and raced down the narrow passageway between the tall metal shelves. The collection of stuff on the shelves looked like a lost and found room at a railway station—but the only thing they were interested in finding were the large parcels of drugs neatly tagged and stored. They grabbed two big caches and stuffed them into their backpacks.

Deputy Dog slipped into the office supply storage room just down the hall from the evidence room. Quickly, he moved around some crates of copier paper and big stacks of computer sheets, building a makeshift hiding place. When the cops found out they had been hit, they would need some clues—something nice and obvious to throw them off the scent. Doubtless, they would speculate that it was here in the storage room that the thieves had hidden waiting to break out to do their dirty work.

The fourth and final number on the electronic combination lock had slotted up on Leedy's computer. The computer room door buzzed quietly and popped open. Ty and Leedy jammed into the room; as they went Earl knocked a piece of paper from a desk. It drifted away to the floor. Neither of them paid attention to it.

Earl Leedy was looking at the big Kray mainframe the way a hungry man stares into a bakery window. In a second he had wired his notebook computer into the big machine and his fingers were flying over the keyboard. The light on the mainframe blinked, then burned steady, indicating access approved.

"Coming right up," said Leedy. "We're making friends here, aren't we, sweetie?" He talked to machines the way he talked to his little kitty cats.

Ty Moncrief spoke into the headset clipped over his cap. "One minute."

Torski was stationed by the elevator bank, watching as the numbers on the display blinked their way up to his floor. "Elevator coming up," he whispered into his headset.

Moncrief registered the message and shot an urgent look over at Leedy. The computer whiz was working like a maniac, crunching the codes as fast as he could. Suddenly he stopped and stared at the screen.

"Got it!" He uncoupled his portable from the mainframe and resealed the computer case.

"We're gone," said Ty. "Let's go."

The elevator stopped on their floor and a female police officer emerged. She was carrying something in a small plastic bag—a piece of evidence that needed to be logged. Torski and Kara were gone, Leedy was following them up the stairs to the roof. Last out was Moncrief. Always the perfectionist, he took one last look around the computer room and picked up the piece of paper, replacing in on the desk—exactly where it had been before Leedy knocked it off.

The female cop suspected nothing out of the ordinary.

She rounded the corner and walked to the evidence cage, surprised to see that no one was on duty at the window. Then she looked down and saw the cop dead on the floor.

Six floors above, Ty Moncrief and his team fanned out on the roof. They had already hooked themselves back into their harnesses and were working toward the edge of the building, stepping out into the abyss without hesitation. They fell a sickening story or two before the wind caught them and carried them along, para-gliding through the dark streets.

Leedy, yoked to Torski, was the last to go over the side. If anything, this was scarier than bailing out of an airplane. At least in a plane you had some advantage of height and speed—velocity to carry you and altitude to give you time to correct any mistakes. Dumping from a building allowed for very little margin for error.

"Oh, God . . . Oh—" Leedy gagged and heaved with fear as Torski ran for the brink.

They didn't have far to go, para-gliding a block or two down the street and landing in the bed of semi-tractor-trailer truck. They hit the truck on the move, and the instant they touched down they threw themselves against the sides of the vehicle. Ty rapped on the bulkhead between the bed and the cab. Deuce hit the gas and the truck picked up speed, zooming through the dark streets, out of the city.

Now they let go, the built-up adrenaline in their veins flooding through them. Kara and Deputy Dog whooped and hollered, pounding each other on the shoulders in celebration, their joyous shouts lost in the roar of the powerful truck engine. Even Ty Moncrief permitted himself a satisfied smile—the operation had been proceeded flawlessly. Just fourteen minutes had passed since they bailed out of the plane and a scant six had actually been spent in the police building. They had gotten in and out and no one was the wiser—not yet anyway. Even Leedy had performed up to expectations.

Only Torski was angry. The instant the truck roared away, he started stripping off his jumpsuit.

"Fuckin Leedy! He threw up on me!"

But he got no sympathy from the rest of the crew. They just laughed and yelled as the truck pounded away through the night.

11

In keeping with the approved skydiver look, Pete hadn't shaved that morning and his hair was a mess. It was a beginning, the first step toward fitting in, to looking like everybody else.

There was a different guard on the gate at the Ocean Reef Drop Zone that morning. Pete drove his Mustang up to the post and rolled down his window. A gale of music from the radio blasted out into the humid morning air.

"I'm dropping this car off for Jessie Crossman," he said, shouting to make himself heard over the music.

Pete's new look must have convinced the guard, who didn't even bother to ask him for a pass. As far as the rent-a-cop was concerned, this was just another grungy, crazy skydiver. He waved him through without a second glance.

Pete parked in the trailer area, got out of the car and started wandering through the drop zone. There was a circus-like atmosphere in the air, as if he had stumbled on a convention of lunatics all out looking for a good time.

The sky was full of divers and planes, parachutists in teams putting their elaborate routines through practice, tightening up performances until they were perfect. Sky-divers were landing on the gravel targets—some as soft as butterflies, others coming in too hot, too fast—and skidding, landing on their asses. They were forced to undergo the good-natured derision of the few onlookers.

Pete wandered over to the packing area and watched as colorful chutes laid out on long wooden tables were being stowed in the bags, carefully and methodically. There was no joking around here—mistakes made in packing cost lives.

On an open area of stubbly grass a team rehearsed routines, a delicate choreography danced on the ground to be executed later in the air. It was not unlike watching a basketball team dry-running their plays on the day before the big game.

The noise from the cool dark cavern of an airplane hangar attracted him and he poked his head in. Standing in the middle of the vast floor space was a vertical wind tunnel, a tube that looked like—and was as wide as—a sawed-off grain silo. The wind tunnel walls were padded, its floor a plastic grid with two huge turbine driven propellers beneath it. They blew a vertical column of air straight up through the tunnel, the props generating enough wind force to send skydivers floating thirty feet above the grate.

Skydivers were practicing free fall positions and aerial gymnastics in the air flow, while an operator watched through an observation window in the base, controlling the force and flow of the air.

Over the tunnel entrance was a stern warning: EMPTY YOUR POCKETS NOW!

A diver about to enter the tunnel was handing over his keys and change to the man in charge of the contraption, a heavily bearded man whom Pete recognized from the night before, a man he had seen in Alabama Jacks. He had been the guy telling the story about skydiving into the middle of some poor suburban bride's wedding.

"This crap gets loose in there and you'll be chewing shrapnel," he said.

"I hear you Late Jake."

Next to the wind tunnel Pete spotted more familiar faces from the night before. Jumpers were standing under a banner that read: FOURTH OF JULY SHOW JUMP. WASHINGTON D.C. TEAM SIGN UP HERE. They were all waiting for their turn at the table to enter the competition. Without thinking about it, Pete joined the line and inched his way forward.

"Hi. I want to sign up for the exhibition."

Kara was standing next to him, waiting for her turn to sign on. "What team are you with?"

"Team?"

"This is a team exhibition, jack. No solos. You with a team or not?"

Torski sidled up to them and looked Pete over, his eyes narrowing as if maybe he had seen him some place before, but couldn't quite figure out where.

"I know you from somewhere."

Pete was genuinely puzzled. He hadn't seen Torski in the confusion of the plane hijack and didn't know the big man from Adam.

Kara thought he looked familiar, but for a different reason. "You're the guy who was with Jess Crossman last night. In the bar, right? You jumped with her?"

"Yeah," said Pete. Well, he reasoned, it was *sort* of true . . .

Torski continued to stare at Pete, as if he had to place him or he wouldn't be able to get to sleep that night. "I never seen you at Ocean Reef before."

"I'm from the West Coast," said Pete. He wished this

big redneck would let it go, but he didn't want to call any more attention to himself than he had already.

"The West Coast, huh?" said Torski, as if he had caught him in a lie. "What part you from?"

"L.A."

"Really?" said Kara. "You know Jack Haney?"

Pete nodded and punted. "Sure. He's a good jumper."

"He's an asshole," countered Torski.

Pete flashed the man a little smile. "You think that—but I don't, but it's probably because I know Jack better than you do."

"That a fact?" said Torski. "He's my brother."

Now Kara was getting suspicious. Skydivers were a tight knit fraternity, a small tribe of risk takers and it seemed apparent that Pete did not fit in. "What kind of rig is it you jump?"

Pete didn't even know how to begin to fudge this question. It looked like he was going to be found out before he even got in the door. "Ah, well . . . I'm going with this, um, custom rig that . . ."

"Oh, just tell them—" The three turned and saw Jessie Crossman coming toward them. "Tell them, they won't be jealous. He jumps a Racer Elite." She slung a black and green Double Vector X parachute off her shoulder and into Pete's arms. "And you left it in the van, Mr. Bucks Deluxe. From now on you carry your own bags."

"Yeah," said Pete. "So there it is. Been looking for that."

Jessie shot a mean look at Kara and Torski. "Why don't you two get the hell out of here?" She shot a look over her shoulder at Pete. "You're screwing with my bankroll."

"Sorry, Jess. . . ." Kara smirked. "I guess we didn't

realize you were fielding a team." She cocked her chin at Pete. "So this roadkill is yours?"

"Yeah."

Kara seemed to be taking this in, nodding to herself, as if digesting the information. Jessie was unprepared for what she said next. "It's real shitty about Jagger, huh?"

Jessie and Kara eyeballed each other, a long history of bad blood hanging in the air between them.

"Yeah," said Jessie. "It is."

The eyes of the two women locked and Jessie wondered if they should get this whole thing over with right now. The antipathy between them was going to come to head eventually, why not right now? Then she felt Pete's hand on her shoulder.

"Come on," he said. "We've got work to do."

Jessie broke away from him. "Kara . . . do you plan on being at the D.C. jump?"

"Bet on it."

"See you up there," said Jessie. Then she walked away, Pete following. All the way to the door, he could feel Torski's curious stare on his back.

"Nice friends you got," Pete mumbled.

"They're good jumpers."

"So what? Is that all that matters? Forgive me, but it seems like a kind of limited view of the world."

"Hey, you wanted into this team, remember? You came to *me* remember?"

"Team? I don't remember saying anything about joining a team."

"Without a team you don't get in the game. Haven't you figured that out yet?"

"And a team takes money, right?"

Jessie nodded. *"Riiight,"* she drawled sarcastically. *"Now* you're catching on."

"Fifteen thousand, right?"

"Right. That's my price. . . ."

"Well, I don't have fifteen goddamned thousand dollars, so I guess I'll have to make do on my own. Okay?"

Jessie hesitated a second. Then she dropped her attitude and got serious. "How much you got?"

She wanted to make it to the Washington, D.C., jump, of course, but there was more to it than that. She wanted to know how Don Jagger had died and somehow she had the feeling that Pete Nessip was going to lead her through that mystery. Of course, she wasn't used to being on the same side with the law. It felt funny, unnatural, and she wasn't sure she cared for it at all.

"How much?" Pete laughed. "If I sell my car and don't eat for two years. . . . Maybe I could come up with seven, maybe, eight thousand."

"That'll do," said Jessie curtly.

Pete looked at her hard, trying to assess this sudden and unexpected change in her attitude. "You know, for someone whose best friend just burned out, or whatever you called it—"

"Burned in."

"Whatever. Seems to me you're damn anxious to get on this exhibition jump up in D.C."

"So what? Do we have a deal?"

"When was the last time you talked to Jagger?"

"I haven't seen him in four months. I don't know what he was doing or who he's been jumping with."

"So why are you here?" Pete demanded. "Why are you even talking to me?"

"I told you. . . . This D.C. gig is the jump of the year. I want to be in on it—and you're my ticket."

Pete looked at her through narrowed eyes. "Why don't I have a good feeling about trusting you?"

Jessie half smiled. "If you had a better idea, you probably wouldn't."

Pete returned the smile—he knew she was right. "So when do I see this team?"

"Simple," she said. "When I see the money."

12

The story of the two murders in the heart of police head-quarters led every newscast in the Miami area. Ty Moncrief sat in front of the television set with the remote control in his hand clicking rapidly from station to station, as if trying to watch all the news broadcasts at once.

The different channels all told the same story and showed the same pictures. As images of the evidence room cage and the blood-stained floor played out on the screen, a grim-sounding reporter gave the facts: that thieves had hidden in the police headquarters building during normal business hours and, once the building was deserted, had emerged from their hiding places to steal cocaine. from the evidence room—but they had not counted on encountering any cops. When they did, the thieves killed them.

The police were reporting that some fifty thousand dollars worth of drugs had been stolen. They had also announced that there was an intense internal affairs review of the case under way.

Ty Moncrief killed the TV set and cackled. "Did you hear that? Did you? Internal affairs review! That means they think that the *cops* may have been involved. They suspect their own." He clapped his hands and rubbed them together vigorously. "Sowing doubt and dissension in the ranks of the Miami PD—not even I had counted on that little bonus."

Leedy looked up from his video display terminal. He had linked his notebook computer to the larger one and was busy playing both keyboards like a virtuoso. The raid on the Miami police department headquarters had been built around this. Leedy had hooked his powerful notebook to the mainframe and had stolen a series of secret files, copying a piece of the big computer on to the hard drive of the smaller one. Now, back in the swamp hideout, he had time to break the access codes and unlock the information he had stolen. He was just about done.

"I have to admit it," he said. "You're good. But so am I. Okay—" He snapped on the laser printer. "Here come your undercovers."

Numbers were scrolling across the screen, then suddenly, everything froze. The VDT divided itself into two halves, a series of photographic images like mug shots appearing in the left hand window, while the data on each materialized on the right.

There were three pictures—a fat-faced Latin man, somewhere in his late twenties; an older, scrawny, bearded white man; and an attractive black woman, who looked as if she was scarcely out of her teens. Leedy examined them for a moment, then set the machine to print, the high-speed printer spitting out copies in a matter of seconds. He handed them over to Moncrief.

"There you go. . . ."

Moncrief took the three pieces of paper and looked at them closely. "How about this? Just think, these narcs are walking around somewhere thinking they're alive. . . ." He popped open his briefcase and dropped in the sheets of paper.

Leedy stood up from the computer and stretched.

"So," he said, his voice full of hope. "Is that it? Am I done?"

Ty Moncrief shook his head. "No, not yet. But it won't be long now—just a few more days."

From outside the house came the sound of an outboard motor, a speedboat drawing up to the old water-logged jetty. Leedy's face contorted in fear. "Who's that coming? Are you expecting anybody?"

"Relax," said Moncrief. "Nothing to worry about. . . . It's just the police."

"The *what*?" Leedy's voice was an alarmed screech and as the door opened he backed away from it.

Moncrief had been telling the truth—it was the police, in the form of Detective Norm Fox. He entered the cabin without saying a word, handed an envelope to Moncrief and received the briefcase in return. In a matter of seconds he was gone.

Ty tore open the envelope and pulled out a photograph. He showed it to Leedy. "This man look familiar? Is this the other Marshal from the plane?"

It was the official United States Marshal Service picture of Pete Nessip, the one the service's office of public information would give out if Pete should ever do anything particularly heroic or get himself killed in the line of duty. In the photo Pete's hair was neatly trimmed, his tie perfectly knotted at his throat, his shirt blindingly white—the very model of a spit and polish law enforcement officer. It was a long way from this to the slovenly, would-be skydiver wandering around the Ocean Reef drop zone that morning. . . .

Leedy felt a sick feeling in the pit of his stomach when he looked at the picture. "Yes. That's him. You said you took care of him."

"Don't worry," said Moncrief lightly.

"Don't *worry*?" Leedy wailed. "You killed his brother, for God's sake!"

"Look," said Ty. "This is how it is. I'll handle my end, Leedy. You worry about yours. . . . But right now, since you've been a good boy, I have a surprise for you. . . ."

"Surprise? What kind of surprise?" Leedy hung back and looked warily at Moncrief. In his experience, surprises from Moncrief tended to have a rather sharp edge to them.

Right on cue, Kara entered the cabin. She was carrying a pet carrier—inside Agnes and Cleo were meowing piteously. Leedy's face lit up. "My babies!"

He tried to grab them, but Ty kept the carrier just out of reach, like a kid playing keep-away. "Keep up the good work, Earl?"

"Yeah. I will."

"Good." He handed over the case full of cats, then turned to Kara and Torski, giving them the picture of Pete.

"Here," he said. "Why don't you lovebirds take a stroll around the drop zone."

Kara stared at the picture, then glanced at Torski. "Crossman's buddy?" she asked.

It took a depressingly brief period of time for Pete Nessip to dispose of all his worldly goods—and when he was finished, the sum of cash he had in hand was disappointingly small. He had a total of eight thousand six hundred dollars, seventy-five hundred of which had come from the sale of his Mustang, the balance coming from his checking account which he had cleaned out and closed down.

He had promised Jessie Crossman a bankroll of eight

thousand which left him with six hundred in hand. He was powerless without transport, so he invested the left-over money in a beat-up motorcycle, a bruised and dented machine, but with a good powerful engine.

In keeping with the skydiver ethos—the more screwed up something is, the better they like it—Jessie Crossman eyed his new motorcycle with profound admiration.

"Cool bike," she said. "Much better than that car of yours."

The subject did not interest him in the slightest. Pete pulled a roll of bills the size of his fist from his pants pocket. "Air time."

Jessie reached for the money, but he pulled his hand back before she could snatch it from his grasp. "Not so fast . . . What about my team?"

Jessie smirked and sniggered. "*Your* team? Mister, you're only *paying* for them. That doesn't make them *yours*."

"Well then show me what my money is buying."

"Come on."

Together they waded into the spectator area. The competition had started in earnest, the sky full of teams of jumpers going through their routines. So the crowd on the ground could see every little maneuver, each team jumped with a cameraman who relayed pictures to the ground and were displayed on big screen televisions scattered around the viewing stands.

Pete's old pals, The Green Team, were in the air going through a very complicated series of drills. Pete was struck by the grace and fluidity of their movements and with how at ease the team members were in the element of rushing air and extreme height. The camera seemed to float around them, catching the skydivers from every angle.

"They looked pretty hot to me," said Pete, genuinely impressed. "Maybe one of these guys will throw in with us. Couldn't hurt, right?"

Jessie merely glanced at the screen. The Green Team wasn't doing anything she hadn't seen before. "They're okay. . . . It's the guy taking pictures you have to watch. He has to be twice as good as everybody else to get tape like that."

A few minutes later the Green Team floated to the ground, each one of the divers hitting the target. Pete still thought they looked pretty good, but Jessie walked straight by them to the cameraman. In place of the usual helmet, the photographer was wearing a Para-Mount Pro Elite helmet camera, a Sony video camera mounted on the crown and a Nikon 35mm still camera positioned on the visor.

"So that's how they do it," said Pete.

"Hey, Bobby!" Jessie walked over to the photographer who was peeling off his helmet. "Nice work."

Bobby beamed. Public praise from Jessie Crossman was quite a feather in anyone's cap. "Thanks, Jess."

"I'm putting together a team for the D.C. jump," said Jessie. "How 'bout it? You interested?"

Bobby beamed. "Hell, yes! Where you been darlin'?" By way of resignation he tossed his helmet to the team leader of the Greens and walked away with Jessie.

"Bobby," Jessie asked, "you seen Swoop around anyplace? I thought I'd run into him here but so far, no luck. . . ."

"Doubt if he's here," said Bobby with a slow shake of his head. "I haven't seen him in a long time. I hear he's living on the streets."

"Well, if he's not here, I think I know where we can

find him," said Jessie. "If we can get Swoop and Hock-ridge then we've got ourselves a team."

But her hopes were dashed almost immediately. Winona and Selkirk walked through the crowd, searching for them.

"Jess," said Winona. "You can forget about Hock-ridge."

"Damn. What? Is he already in a team?"

"Worse. He busted his ankle."

Selkirk laughed. "And it wasn't even on a jump . . . The klutz was getting out of the bathtub. . . ."

"That is bad news," said Jessie. "Real bad news." She looked at Winona. "Now what the hell do we do?"

"Well," said Selkirk casually. "I figure I can fill in, no problem." The mechanic shrugged and sniffed like it was no big deal—he was trying so hard to be as cool as possible that he was coming off awkward and shy.

Jessie barely considered his kind offer. "What have you logged?" she asked dismissively. "Must be a whole—what?—twenty jumps."

Selkirk dropped the cool act. "Thirty jumps, Jess. Thirty. And when was the last time you watched me jump, huh? You might be impressed, you know?"

Jessie folded her arms across her chest. "I doubt it."

Winona felt compelled to jump in. "Jessie, he's look-ing pretty good. I've been giving him . . . a lot of extra air time lately."

"Yeah," said Selkirk boastfully. "Let me show you, Jess. I can slice the sky to pieces."

Jessie was unmoved by his swagger. "Look, kid, I don't need Indiana Jones. I need somebody who's good and who can take orders."

"Look," said Selkirk. "If I can't cut it, I'll find some-body who can."

Pete figured it was his money that was financing all this, so he had a say in who got hired. Of all the people he had met so far, Selkirk was the one who had helped him the most and now he deserved a break. "Hey," he said. "I like his attitude. The kid's got some enthusiasm."

Jessie looked at Pete with disdain, as if he was some lower form of non-skydiving life. "Enthusiasm can get you killed up there."

"You want me to call Burt?" Winona asked. "He could probably be here by next week."

"Next week? No way. We don't have that kind of time. . . ." She took a long hard look at Selkirk as if seeing him for the first time. "Okay kid, here's the drill. Three conditions: first of all, you're still a mechanic. Your main job is to keep the plane flying. Second, if you hot dog on me—you're gone. No warnings, no probation, just bye-bye. Got it?"

"Got it. What's the third thing?"

"Third, you watch out about that . . . extra air time."

Like a man more or less resigned to his fate, Selkirk nodded—but the instant Jessie turned her back to him, he jumped a foot in the air, pumped his fist and shouted—"*YES!*"

With the team—such as it was—beginning to take shape, Jessie realized that there was little time to waste. "Winona, crank the plane up. Let's go find Swoop."

Pete stopped her. "What about me?"

Jessie shrugged. "I guess you can come too. There's enough room. . . ."

"I don't mean that. I mean about jumping. Joining this team you're building."

"You? Jumping?" She shook her head. "Uh-uh.

You're no good to me dead. I need you alive to deal with my probation officer.''

''But I'm serious.''

''So am I.'' She wasn't kidding him now. ''I'm a good teacher, but there's nobody so good that they could get you up to exhibition level in a week.''

Pete really didn't give a damn about skydiving, the exhibition, or anything connected with this crazy sport. He was in hock and involved for one reason—and one reason only. He wanted to find the person who killed Terry and if that meant jumping out of an airplane, so be it.

''Jessie,'' he said. ''Here's the drill. Something tells me I'm not going to find who I'm looking for on the ground. Either I jump or we don't have a deal. Got it?''

Jessie got it. ''Okay, but you're an alternate.''

''Alternate what?''

''You train, but you don't jump the exhibition. That's the offer. You in or out?''

''I'm in.''

''Then let's go. . . .''

Halfway to the airfield they ran into Kara. She looked at Jessie, a challenge in her eyes. ''What's this I hear about Selkirk jumping with you and Mr. Los Angeles over there?'' She cocked her chin at Pete. ''What happened? Did you lose a bet or something?''

''You know me,'' said Jessie. ''I've never been afraid of a challenge.''

Kara laughed. ''Maybe you should just throw in with us and save yourself the aggravation.''

''Really? Tell me who else you have on your team. I'm kind of particular about who I jump with, you know.''

''Really? I never would have guessed.'' Kara looked over at Pete—it was obvious she wouldn't name names

109

in front of strangers. Pete looked away, the idiosyncracies of skydivers were really beginning to get on his nerves.

"Just trust me, Jessie," said Kara. "These guys are good. Very good."

"Well, I've got some good guys on my team, too, Kara."

The woman snorted and looked at Pete. "Who? Him?"

"Bobby," said Jessie. "And Swoop. . . . So I guess as far as your offer goes . . . maybe some other time."

Jessie started toward the plane. Both Pete and Kara watched her go, both of them wondering the same thing. It was hard to tell what Jessie was up to, where her thinking was going. But Pete and Kara wanted to know which side of the fence was she playing. And whose side was she really on.

13

When Kara and Torski returned to Moncrief's base of operations in the swamp, they found him working over a parachute rig, doing a little light maintenance with a gadget called a nylon punch. The implement looked like a staple gun, but instead of firing staples, it punched holes in the dense mass of nylon rigging. In the background, Deputy Dog pumped some small barbells, working on his upper arms, keeping up his strength. In a corner Leedy fussed with his cats.

Moncrief hardly looked up from his rig. "What did you find out?"

"He's here," said Kara. "The guy is hanging with Jessie Crossman. She's putting together one hell of a half-assed team."

"Who are they?" asked Moncrief. "Anybody I know?"

"Naww," said Torski. "Nothing but sky junkies . . . and a couple of wannabes. Not a thing for us to worry about."

Leedy picked up his cat, the one called Agnes and looked into her eyes. He appeared to be as concerned as a parent with a sick infant.

"This humidity is just awful for the cats," he clucked. "I have got to get them to a vet."

Ty shot a dirty look in his direction. Leedy was really getting on his nerves—it was a shame he was so essential to the operation. Next time he would find himself a computer expert with a less grating personality. Next time . . .

"What are you going to do, boss?" asked Deputy Dog, still pumping the weights. "I say let's take this marshal out so we don't have to worry about him anymore. No marshal—no problem."

Leedy was paying no attention to the discussion. He was far more interested in his cats.

"This marshal, this Nessip. He's on suspension," said Ty. He fired the nylon punch, piercing the fabric on the table in three places. "The higher-ups yanked his badge. They don't like him and they don't trust him. He's a loose cannon."

"Yeah?" said Torski. "So what?"

Ty looked at Torski with a little pity in his eyes—Moncrief was very glad that he did the thinking for this outfit. "So, if we take him out, whatever theory it was he couldn't sell to his bosses will suddenly start making sense to them. Right now they just think he's crazy."

"So what do we do?" asked Kara.

"Nothing," said Moncrief emphatically. "Absolutely nothing. We act like every other team in the sky—we train for the exhibition."

"You know," said Leedy. "I really can't be going anywhere until I get my cats to a vet. I'm terribly sorry, but that's just the way it is. . . ."

If he expected Ty Moncrief to announce that training was suspended and the operation postponed indefinitely pending a clean bill of health for Agnes and Cleo, Earl Leedy was terribly mistaken. It also showed that he had not really gotten to know Ty Moncrief terribly well.

Moncrief's hand shot out and grabbed Leedy by the

neck. He slammed the man's head down on the work-table, pressed the nylon punch against Leedy's earlobe and fired, popping a hole clean through the flesh.

"We follow my schedule," said Moncrief. "As planned."

He hardly glanced at Leedy. Blood was streaming down his neck and there was a look of absolute shock in his pale eyes—he was so stunned that the pain hadn't even registered in his brain yet.

Moncrief pulled a hundred dollar bill from his jeans and threw it at Leedy. "Here. Go buy yourself an ear-ring."

Jessie Crossman's DC 3 airplane cruised northeast from Ocean Creek, Winona relaxed and confident behind the controls. An hour into the flight, she pushed forward on the yoke and the plane lost altitude, a fast circle that burned a couple of thousand feet.

It was obvious to Pete that they were preparing to land. He looked out the window, scanning the ground below, searching for the air field. But he couldn't see one—the only really noticeable feature of the landscape was a long, wide bridge traversing a deep gorge. The water of a narrow river sparkled in the valley beneath far down beneath the bridge.

The plane was descending toward the span. There was very little traffic on the road and Pete leaned to Jessie and smiled. "Almost looks like Winona is planning on landing on that bridge down there."

"Yeah," said Jessie. "Funny, huh?"

"I'm getting used to you guys," said Pete. "Nothing would surprise me."

"Good."

The plane lost another couple of hundred feet.

"Why?"

"Because we *are* landing on the bridge."

"Say what!" Pete threw himself against the window, flattening himself against the Plexiglas, staring down at the bridge. A couple of cars were travelling across the span, but Winona continued to push the plane down, as if she didn't see them or was confident that they would make way for a nice big airplane. "Is she crazy?"

Meanwhile, Jessie had brought Pete to a building in downtown Miami to "look for someone." But when they got to the roof, a vast square of concrete bristling with antennae and transponder dishes, it was empty of people.

Pete shook his head. "Why're we up here?"

Jessie didn't answer. "Swoop!"

"I said, why are we up here?"

"We're looking for Swoop."

"I figured that part out already. Who's Swoop?"

"Swoop is the best. He's a little weird, but he can do anything with a parachute rig except knit you a sweater. If we can get him to join us then we're going to D.C. for sure."

"Okay," said Pete. "Now I know."

Jessie threw herself up on the parapet that lined the edge of the building and looked down at the streets below. Cautiously, Pete peered over—the sheer drop was enough to make him feel queasy.

"Swoop!" Jessie yelled again.

"Right here."

They craned over the edge and looked down. Directly below them was Swoop, standing in a window washer's rig. He was about thirty, lean and muscular and dressed in a dirty, paint-stained denim's overalls and little else. In his hands he held a plastic Windex bottle filled with filthy water and an even filthier rag. He shot a wild, slightly crazy grin at his unexpected visitors.

"What you doing down there, Swoop?" Jessie asked.

Swoop shrugged. "I thought they might like their windows washed."

Pete definitely got the impression that "a little weird" was something of a understatement.

"I need you for a team," said Jessie.

"Any money in it?"

Jess shook her head. "Nope. Nothing. Not one thin dime. Sorry."

Swoop shrugged and spritzed a little dirty water on the already streaked glass. He rubbed the damp spot vigorously with the rag, shaking his head as he did so. It was plain that he wasn't coming off that rig any time soon.

Pete took a crack at changing his mind. "All your jumps are paid for," he said.

But it was as if Swoop hadn't heard him. He ignored Pete completely, speaking to Jessie as if Pete wasn't even within earshot.

"So how about the jumps, Jess," he asked. "Are they paid for or what?"

"I just told you they were," said Pete. "Didn't you hear me?"

Swoop appeared to be selectively deaf. He could hear Jess perfectly, but Pete Nessip might as well have been in another state. His words made no impression on Swoop at all.

"Yep," said Jessie. "The air time is all free. Got myself a backer"—she shot a sidelong glance at Pete—"a real deep pocket."

"No shit," said Swoop.

"It's me," said Pete. "Those are my pockets she's talking about."

115

"Who's the lucky guy?" Swoop asked, still speaking directly to Jessie.

Jessie jerked a thumb at Pete. "Him."

"Just what the hell is going on here?" asked Pete.

"Just a little quirk of Swoop's," Jessie explained. "If he hasn't jumped with you, he won't talk to you. Don't worry about it."

"I'm not worried. It's just really annoying."

"Yeah, well," said Jessie with a laugh, "that's Swoop."

"Hey, Jess, we get free T-shirts?"

Jessie looked at Pete. "I don't know. Do we?"

Pete shrugged. "Yeah, sure . . . whatever you want."

"Sure," said Jessie. "Lots of free T-shirts."

"Well . . . okay." Swoop started climbing out of the rig, oblivious to the nightmare vista below him. He stretched out an arm. "Gimme a hand, would ya, Jess?"

He reached for her, but in a split second he seemed to lose his balance, his arms windmilling in the air. A look of pure terror crossed his face—a look mirrored in Pete's face.

"Jesus Christ! He's going over!"

Pete lunged, but before he could reach him, Swoop fell backwards tumbling into the abyss, screaming in terror as he tumbled.

"Oh my God!" Pete wanted to look away, but he could not tear his eyes from the horrific scene. Swoop was dropping like a lead weight toward the hard sidewalk below, surely to be smashed to pieces on the unforgiving concrete. Pete felt sick in the pit of his stomach.

Then the pilot chute from the rig Swoop was wearing popped out and the canopy deployed, a splash of bright red in the middle of the office tower canyons. Pete watched as Swoop floated down into the busy Miami traffic.

Pete did his best to calm his racing pulse. "Tell me," he gasped. "I thought you said he was a *little* weird."

Jessie considered this for a moment. "Swoop's got a funny sense of humor, that's all."

"I figured," said Pete. "And it's just my luck—he's on *my* team."

14

They were back at the Ocean Reef drop zone by nightfall, Pete wandering over to the team mobile home that Selkirk had parked in the campground area of the exhibition site. He pulled a beer out of a little refrigerator and sat on the steps of the RV, sipping the cold brew and thinking about the events of the day. Things were quiet around the drop zone—the competition was finished for the day and virtually all the teams were down at Alabama Jacks getting as wasted as they could afford.

Pete was so deep in thought that he couldn't be sure whether he had actually seen someone moving out of the corner of his eye or if he had imagined it. He looked up and saw that someone, a man or a woman, was stealthily creeping across the clearing, making for one of the old hangars which served as an equipment shop.

Pete put down his beer and followed silently. The figure had jimmied open a little window in the side of the building and slipped inside. An instant later a flashlight lit up a pool of light within, going from parachute to parachute.

On a worktable at the rear of the shop was the object of the search. It was a parachute rig marked with a large yellow police tag.

"Find what you're looking for?"

Jessie whipped around, fixing the flashlight beam on Pete.

"Jesus!" she said. "How long have you been fucking following me?"

"Ever since you decided to be my friend," Pete replied. "What's this all about anyway?"

Jessie sighed. "When a skydiver burns in, the cops bring the rig to an area safety officer for inspection." She swung the beam of the flashlight around till it rested on the pile of black fabric. "This is Don Jagger's."

"And?"

"And there's nothing wrong with this rig, not a damn thing. Which means he would have had to screw up big time to go into the power lines. And there's no way that happened. . . ."

"You're sure of that?"

"The man was a world champion," said Jessie. "For him to go into power lines . . . that's a mistake that you just don't make when you're as good as he was." Jessie shook her head. "I think he had help."

Pete walked over and took a closer look at Don Jagger's parachute rig. He had seen a lot of parachutes in the last few days, but they still more or less looked the same to him. But there was something different about this rig—even he could see it.

The Navy SEAL commander Dejaye had pointed out the D rings on a parachute rig—he had said they were made of high density steel that would trip any metal detector. Pete fingered the rings.

"I thought these things were supposed to be made out of metal," he said.

"This one is high density fabric," Jessie explained. "That makes it a smuggler's rig."

"A what?"

119

"Drug runners custom-make these things. It helps them avoid the radar. There's no metal in the whole rig. If there isn't any metal, then there's no radar profile."

Pete felt a tingle of excitement. "So you could get one of these things through airport security, right?"

"You got it."

He pulled a pocket knife from his pants pocket and carved a small piece of fabric off the D ring. "Make sure you put this rig back just the way it was."

"Okay."

"And remember something—these people don't care who they kill, Crossman, so from here on in leave the cop stuff to me. Understand?"

Jessie looked him in the eye. "Seeing you in a jump-suit might be enough to scare them to death," she said evenly.

"Seeing you in a bathing suit might do the same thing," Pete responded with a smirk as she turned and walked away. Pete watched her for a moment, then headed back to his trailer.

Mike Milton's laboratory in the Department of Justice building in Washington D.C. was so crammed with high end computer and forensic equipment that it looked like science-geek Shangri-la. The place was so perfectly set up that Milton—who, to be honest, didn't have much of a life outside of his job—hardly ever left.

When Pete called the lab from Ocean Reef that night, he was pretty confident that he would find Mike there—even though it was almost midnight and Milton was the only person in the building except for a bunch of sleepy security guards and some of the cleaning crew.

Mike was not working. Even he got tired sometimes. He was slumped in his rolling desk chair, his feet propped on the old sofa in his office, head back, mouth open, sound asleep and snoring slightly.

When the phone rang, Mike jerked upright, the chair sliding out from underneath him, sending him to the hard floor of the room with a crash. Still woozy from sleep and his abrupt awakening, it took him a moment to figure out the exact location of the ringing phone.

"Yes . . . what? Hello?"

"Wake up, Mikey. It's Nessip. . . ."

Mike Milton was still dazed, his neck was stiff from his awkward sleeping position and he was having trouble getting his eyes to focus. He really should start going home at quitting time like everyone else. . . .

"Hey, Mike!" Pete shouted down the line, trying to shock his old friend into consciousness. "I said, wake up!"

"Yeah, okay. I'm awake." He rubbed his eyes vigorously. "Pete? Is that you?"

"Yeah, Mike. Now listen carefully . . . ready?"

"Ready."

Pete spoke fast. "I'm having an envelope delivered with a piece of material in it—I think it's nylon. I need to have it analyzed for explosives. Understand?"

Mike was still slightly befuddled. "Explosives . . . nylons?" He wiped his face with his hand and tried to focus his eyes. "What? Are you dating that Mongolian feminist again? Is that it?"

Pete didn't have time to joke around. "Listen to me, Mike," he said soberly. "I really need your help."

"My help?" said Milton. "I heard you were on suspen—vacation."

"Oh yeah, vacation. Life is sweet, you know . . . Mike, it's because I'm on 'vacation' that you have to do this for me. If you don't, I may be on vacation permanently.

That's why I need this piece of material analyzed, understand?''

"No."

"Good. Better that way," said Pete. "I'm overnighting it to you. You should have it by tomorrow—run every test there is, Mike: explosives, alloys, trace particles—the works. Got it?"

"Pete," said Mike. "I think you may be forgetting something crucial. . . ."

"What?" Pete's heart sunk—he was sure that Mike was about to hit him with some polysyllabic reason why nylon couldn't be analyzed for explosives.

"This is the Justice Department," said Mike. "We don't have time for things like that. I'm booked solid. We have bigger fish to fry—we're taking Tonya to trial next week."

"Mike, please. Do this for me," Pete pleaded. "I wouldn't ask, except it's my only way back in."

"Look, Pete—I'm not kidding. I don't have the time for this. I'm sorry."

"Well, there must be *someone* in that lab who can do it. It's important. . . ."

"I gathered." Milton sighed. "I could ask Luxem to do it. He's not so busy this week."

"Can he keep a secret?"

"Uh-huh."

"Then he's our man. . . ." Pete paused. "But, Mike, you should tell your buddy don't let anyone know it's for me or they'll fire your ass, and his and mine. Got it?"

"Got it."

Only a few short moments before, Mike Milton, peacefully dozing away, did not have a care in the world. Now he was involved in an investigation outside US Marshal Service channels and was being begged by a suspended agent to use government time, money, and materials to run illegal tests on evidence that had probably been obtained in an . . . unorthodox manner. Mike Milton realized he had been taught a very valuable lesson—that answering the phone late at night is always a bad idea.

"Pete?"

"Yeah?"

"Why can't you just be calling to borrow money, like usual?"

The first day of practice did not begin in the air, or even in the wind tunnel, but in a classroom. Jessie showed her team a series of videotapes, footage taken at meets all over the country—all over the world—performances of the finest skydiving performances any of them had ever seen.

The teams on the tapes were flawless, but they had been working together for years and their virtuosity in the air represented thousands of jumps and hundreds of hours of flight time. Jessie was realistic—her own team would never begin to approach serious contention. There wasn't the time or the money for that. The best she could hope for was getting them into shape, getting them in the air, and managing to avoid outright humiliation in front of the cream of the North American skydiving community.

Of course, the competition in Washington D.C. was of only secondary importance. Jessie Crossman wanted to know who killed her former lover and friend, just as much as Pete Nessip wanted to avenge the death of his brother.

From the classroom they moved on to creepers, carpet-covered oversized skateboards, like the rolling boards that auto mechanics use to work on the underside of a car.

Each member of the team lay belly down on their creeper, sliding in and out of formation on Jessie's command, simulating on the ground the series of maneuvers they would be performing in the air.

They were coming along well—much better and faster than Jessie had dared to hope. Of course, Swoop and Bobby were experienced skydivers, so there wasn't too much to worry about there; Selkirk was not as seasoned as the other two, but he had been around drop zones and sky divers for a couple of years and had a basic understanding and vocabulary—plus he had enthusiasm to burn.

The problem was Pete. He was clumsy, he was slow—he was out of his depth. When they worked on the creepers everything looked fine until Pete attempted to move into his position. Like a dancer with two left feet on a crowded floor, he bumped and crashed and pushed everyone else out of formation.

He knew he was bad and so did his teammates, but they didn't ride him or tease him too much—after all, he was paying for all of them and they knew that Jessie would heap more than enough scorn on Pete.

She was merciless, driving them all to work harder and faster, taking them through the maneuvers time and again, until they figured they knew them forwards and backwards.

One by one they spent hours in the wind tunnel, going through a series of freefall positions and aerial gymnastics while Jessie watched and shouted instructions. Winona would circle with a video camera and afterwards, Jessie would go over every inch of tape, criticizing and analyzing, like a coach with game films.

Swoop excelled in the wind tunnel and Bobby was no slouch either. Selkirk was coming along nicely. But Pete, like the class dunce, was pitiful. The first time he got in the tunnel he couldn't do anything, he just sat on that column of air, like a ping pong ball held in the air by a blow drier. His performance would have been funny if it hadn't been so pathetic. . . .

No one realized it except for Pete, but during their first dive as a team he experienced a major breakthrough.

The jump began in a normal enough manner. Winona took them up, the skydivers sitting around the passenger compartment, doing what they always did before a jump. Bobby checked his equipment, unflappable Swoop slouched in a corner reading a comic book and blowing big pink bubbles from a wad of gum in his cheek, Selkirk so pumped up, so psyched he was nearly jumping out of his skin. Pete was sitting in a corner, uncertain about the whole enterprise—apprehensive about the jump, yet at the same time he was bored and tired—he was sick of worrying about skydiving. Suddenly, grabbing the hijackers of Flight 611, the people who had murdered his brother and fourteen others, seemed like a goal a long way off.

Bobby elbowed Pete in the ribs. "Hey, I been meaning to ask you. . . . How many times have you jumped, Nessip?"

Swoop had put down his comic book and was waiting for him to reply. Even Selkirk had managed to contain himself long enough to listen. Pete didn't answer—he didn't know how to break it to him, although he should have seen this moment coming and have been ready for it.

"Yeah," shouted Selkirk. "How many times? Like two thousand maybe?"

"One," said Pete firmly.

Selkirk and the other two nodded at each other. "A thousand jumps. . . . Not bad. In fact, that's pretty good." The whole group looked pleasantly surprised. Just because Nessip was a klutz on the ground didn't mean he would be a screwup in the air.

Bobby shot him a thumbs up. "A thousand jumps. That's great. That means we can depend on you. . . ."

Nessip grimaced. That was the last damn thing he wanted. He decided to come clean. "Uh . . . not one thousand." He held up his index finger. "One. Once. One jump." He shrugged apologetically. "That's all."

"Once!" Bobby shouted. "Jesus!"

Swoop was so disgusted that he could barely chew his bubble gum—and everybody looked at Jessie. Jessie, wisely, looked away. She knew that they were wondering what the hell she had gotten them into—but she also knew she couldn't tell them.

Winona leaned out of the cockpit, signalling a jump run. "We're at altitude."

Jessie stood and walked to the open door, then looked back at her group. Only Selkirk seemed up for the jump. Bobby, Swoop, and Pete stood, their shoulders slumped, like kids condemned to an afternoon of detention.

"Hey!" she shouted, clapping her hands. "Look alive! Are we going or not?"

Selkirk nearly jammed through the roof, but the others followed as if they were going to the gallows. Pete was second after Selkirk, then Swoop followed by Bobby. Jessie brought up the rear. She watched her team and groaned into the rushing wind. They were a mess. . . .

Swoop was doing okay, but he was off on his own hotdogging through the air, as if he was a free-styler or sky-surfer. Selkirk was falling too fast, Bobby was dropping too slow. Pete was as ungainly as a sack of bricks, falling through the air his arms and legs waving in the wind. He looked terrible and was completely out of position—but it was right then, in the middle of that clumsy drop that Pete experienced his breakthrough, his skydiving epiphany.

With a shock he noticed that he wasn't afraid anymore. It was as if the cool refreshing air had carried away his apprehension. The terror had passed and the thrill had overtaken him. He had discovered the exhilaration of the jump, the heady euphoria that came with the sensation of flying.

The jump was all work for Jessie. She carved through the sky, corralling her errant team members like a sheep-dog, nudging and cajoling, pushing them into formation. It was testament to her skill alone that they were able to get into some kind of configuration before they had to break and pull their cords for a landing.

The rest of the team was on the ground before Pete. He came in for his landing fast and heavy, making a rough but survivable touch down. He hit and teetered for a minute before falling down in a heap of arms and legs and billowing cloth.

But he didn't care. The thrill was still pumping through him like a drug. Swoop offered him a hand up, pulling him to his feet.

"That was incredible!" Pete shouted. "That was great! Absolutely wonderful!" He turned to Swoop. "Tell me honestly, how was I?"

Swoop gave him a little look and walked away without answering him. Pete looked over at Bobby.

"Hey, I've jumped with him now. I thought he'd talk after that . . . what's the deal?"

Bobby grinned. "Man, he doesn't count what you just did as a jump!"

Peter shook his head. "Man, I can't win, can I?"

The boogie at Ocean Reef had come to an end and Jessie had made the decision to move her team back to her home drop zone, Sugarloaf. The facilities weren't as good, but they were private and away from prying eyes, and because Jessie owned the field and everything on it, the price was just right.

The first thing Pete did when he returned to Sugarloaf was call Mike Milton in Washington. To make sure that his call wasn't overheard by the rest of the team, he took his cellular phone outside, strolling onto the runway as he talked.

"So Mike, what you got?"

"I'm impressed, Pete. I really am. . . . My buddy Luxem ran the lab on your piece of nylon and he finds out that this is serious guacamole."

"How serious?"

"C-4 explosive," said Milton. "That serious enough for you? Plus magnesium flash-bang residue, high grade alloys—interesting stuff. And you ain't dealing with a cat burglar, Pete."

Pete couldn't say he was happy about these results, but he was quietly, grimly satisfied that his theory was beginning to pan out. "Thanks, Mike," he said. "Tell your friend I owe him big time."

"That's okay. I've taken care of it."

"Taken care of it? How?"

"Easy," said Mike. "I promised him you'd paint his house this summer. . . ."

Peter laughed and pocketed his phone, walking back toward the cluster of buildings at the far end of the runway. Bobby, Swoop, Winona and Selkirk were sitting in folding chairs on the deserted practice field. A cooler of beer stood in the middle of the circle of chairs.

"So where's Jessie?" Pete asked.

Winona cocked her head. "In the office. She's working a little late."

Pete dug a cold beer out of the icy water in the cooler and popped it open.

"How good were Jessie and Jagger?" Selkirk asked. "I never got to see them jump together."

"They were the best," said Bobby with great conviction. "Absolutely the best. Three world championships between them."

Peter looked skeptical. "Really? That good, huh?"

"That's right."

"So why did she jump drugs with him?" Pete asked. "Doesn't make sense."

"She didn't," said Winona.

"Well, she didn't do two years in the joint just for being a smart ass," said Pete.

"She got time because she wouldn't turn evidence on Jagger," Bobby explained. "The judge didn't understand that."

"Yeah," said Pete. "Judges are funny that way."

Winona finished a beer and crushed the thin aluminum can in one hand. "What really sucked was the DEA cut some kind of deal with Jagger and he got out in six months. Jessie they leave in the bucket for her entire jail term. Now that hardly seems fair to me."

A look of puzzlement crossed Pete's face. "Then I don't get it. Jagger sounds like bad news to me—so how come she has all this loyalty to him?"

Winona laughed dryly. "They spent ten years jumping together. I guess that means something to Jessie."

Pete glanced over at the office, then slowly, achingly, got to his feet. "Well," he said. "I'll see you tomorrow. . . ."

Jessie was sitting at her desk staring at a stack of bills, as if she could make them disappear if she concentrated hard enough. She looked up when Pete tapped at the door and almost smiled at him—his warmest welcome yet.

"I just wanted to tell you," Pete said. "I got it today . . . the skydiving. It finally made sense to me."

"I'm afraid to ask. . . ."

"No," he said. "Really . . . I figured it out. You know what the real danger is?"

Jessie nodded. "Yeah. The real danger is the chute won't open."

"Wrong. It's not wanting it to open. I wanted to fly forever."

"Forever comes in a hurry if you think that way."

"But that's not what scares me. . . . What *really* scares me is that I'm starting to understand you."

"Don't get insane on me, Nessip." Her mouth twitched. She seemed to have edged nearer to giving him a real smile.

In that moment, he actually had the feeling she might level with him, tell him what was really on her mind. "So maybe it's time you're straight with me about what you're doing."

"Simple. I'm doing what you paid for. I'm giving you cover."

It was cards on the table time, he decided. "Jagger's rig was laced with the same explosives that were found on that 747. Which means I'm in the right place. And

I don't want you messing me up by trying to settle a grudge.''

Jessie wasn't smiling anymore. "You take care of your problems," she said with a dismissive shrug. "I take care of my own. How's that?"

"Not good enough. These people came from your world," said Pete firmly. "But they made the mistake of crossing into mine. You only want one of them. I want them all. Remember that. . . .''

15

The motor yacht Halcyion, a vessel the size of a small ocean liner, steamed through the calm seas of the Straits of Florida, a few miles north of the Fowey Light. But the vessel was not at sea for a pleasure cruise—far from it. The Halcyion, safe in international waters, was to be the setting for a business meeting between Ty Moncrief and the shadowy employer of Schuster Stevens and Walsh Mathews, a man known only as Mr. Roslund.

A slick looking A-Star chopper had picked up Ty and Kara at the Miami airport and then zoomed out over the water searching for the home base on the helipad of the Halcyion. They touched down fifteen minutes after they took off.

Stephens and Mathews were standing by to greet the two new arrivals and to conduct them down to a lower deck where Mr. Roslund himself waited. As they walked through the ship, Ty glanced around, noting that there seemed to be a goon with an automatic weapon at every corner. Mr. Roslund, it seemed, took his security precautions seriously.

The big boss himself was rather a surprise. Ty had half-expected a young man, a smooth drug dealer full of macho swagger. But Roslund was an elderly, avuncular man, well dressed but not showy. He looked like a prosperous doctor or company executive, the kind of fellow that played a good game of golf at the local club and was a pillar of his community.

There were no pro-forma greetings.

"I promised you a free sample. Here it is." Ty tossed a copy of that morning's Miami Herald on the table in front of the three men. They glanced at the three photographs above the fold on page one—the two men and one woman that Leedy had spirited out of the central police computer—and the headline: UNDERCOVER NARCS KILLED.

Mathews and Schuster smiled. "Yes," said Schuster, "we had heard about this. Most impressive."

Ty smiled. "Thank you." Although he had once been a member of the Drug Enforcement Agency, he didn't seem at all concerned about giving up a trio of law enforcement officers to drug thugs like Roslund and company.

"We've tested your free sample and decided we want more," said Walsh Mathews.

"You understand that from here on it's greenbacks the rest of the way?"

"Your price is rather large," said Stevens. It couldn't hurt to haggle.

"So is my dick but I'm not about to change it," Ty shot back.

"Twenty million dollars?" said Mathews. "That must be some d—"

Moncrief cut him off. "For what you're getting twenty million is a K-Mart special as far as I'm concerned. I'm sure you're not the only . . . businessmen interested in what I have to offer."

Roslund cut right through the back chat. "I'm only interested in long-term investments. What happens when the DEA replaces their dead agents? And they will."

133

"What you're buying is a data service," Kara explained. "Once we're in, we're in . . . and we update your information whenever they do."

"And the charge for this update?" Roslund asked.

"Two million dollars a month for the names and operations of every undercover DEA agent in the world."

"It all sounds wonderful," said Stevens skeptically. "But the question is how."

Ty smirked. "Does Ford tell Chrysler? I don't think so . . ." Enough of dealing with flunkies, he thought. Moncrief looked Roslund in the eye. "Twenty million—five hundred thousand now for expenses. Do we have a deal or not?"

Roslund was silent. Ty looked at Kara and together they turned to go.

"The things they don't teach you at Harvard Business School," said Roslund chuckling. "Schuster . . ." Stevens picked up his cordovan hide briefcase and handed it to Moncrief.

"There you go, Mr. Moncrief," said Roslund. "This is the money for your expenses. When do we see the list?"

Ty hefted the suitcase in his hand, feeling its weight, the satisfying mass and poundage of serious money. "Three days from now," he said. "The fifth of July."

One moment Pete was asleep, the next he was wide awake, his Beretta in his hand. He had been sleeping in a corner of Jessie's living room with the rest of Jessie's team, dead to the world, when a gentle voice awakened him.

Recognizing Jessie, Pete sighed with relief and put down the gun. "Scared the shit out of me. . . ." He raked his fingers through the growth of beard on his chin.

Jessie seemed unfazed by the handgun. "You know, you are really making progress as a skydiver," she said.

The sudden praise was unexpected and Pete drank it up eagerly. "You think so?"

"Yeah . . . I mean, you may not be able to jump like a skydiver but at least you look like one. Seen any coffee?"

Pete pointed to a cabinet, then got up to examine himself in the mirror. He looked terrible, a far cry from the clean-cut Pete Nessip who had appeared at his brother's funeral.

"Will it blow my cover if I take a shower?"

Jessie shook her head. "Don't do it. You're just starting to look good." She handed him a copy of the Miami Herald. "Thought you might want to see this."

"What is it?"

Jessie displayed the front page, the same three photographs of the unfortunate DEA agents. "I thought you might want to consider another line of work. Seems to me, all of a sudden, jumping out of airplanes is a day at the beach compared to some other jobs."

Pete stared at the article, reading it quickly, shaking his head as he took in the details of the brutal murders. It was plain as day that they had been slaughtered because their true identities and purposes had been found out. The paper didn't spell it out, but there was no doubt in Pete's mind that the three had not died quickly and painlessly. . . .

"I don't get it," said Jessie. "The newspaper says that they were so deep undercover that no one was supposed to know they existed. They must have made a mistake. . . ."

"Three DEA agents all make a mistake?" said Pete

skeptically. "When you're under that deep you don't make mistakes. Like Jagger and his power lines . . ."

Pete read the news story to the bottom of the column, then followed the jump to the inside pages where the story finished. Beneath that was a follow-up on the killings of the two Miami cops in the police station heist. The headline told the whole story: MIAMI POLICE STATION ROBBERY BAFFLES INVESTIGATORS.

The news item meant nothing to him at first, so he started to put the paper down. Then he stopped and scanned the article more closely. A lot of cops were turning up dead. . . . And the circumstances were quite unusual.

"Better get ready," said Jessie. "No time for sitting around reading the paper. We've got a long drive up to D.C. today. We're gonna have to drive in shifts. It's about an eighteen-hour drive."

Pete crumpled the paper and tossed it aside. He was hot on the trail of an idea. "You're driving," he said.

"What the hell are you going to be doing?" she asked, irate. Getting a skydiving team packed and on the road was no simple undertaking.

"Me?" he said. "I'm working."

They hit the road a little after nine, all of their gear stowed in Jessie's camper and in a trailer they were pulling. They even found room for Pete's beat-up motorcycle, lashing the machine to the bike frame on the rear of the vehicle.

They had just made it on to the interstate when Winona flew over in the plane, just above treetop height, rocking her wings in recognition before circling once and then putting her nose to the north.

Pete grimaced. "Why didn't *I* hitch a ride with her?"

He did not relish being cooped up in a camper for the

136

better part of twenty-four hours, particularly with a bunch of skydivers—their lack of concern about personal hygiene could become a bit trying after even a very short period of time.

Jessie, at the wheel, looked into the rearview mirror, fixing Pete in her gaze. "Hey, you told me you had a lot of work to do, ace. No one's going to disturb you."

"I appreciate it." Pete moved to the very rear of the camper, locking himself in the tiny bedroom cabin and pulling out his cellular phone. He pumped in the number for the Justice Department lab and a few seconds later a familiar voice filled the earpiece.

"Mike Milton."

"Mike . . ." Pete cackled. "How would you like me to paint *your* house."

Mike's voice dropped in volume, as if someone was listening over his shoulder. He spoke just above a whisper. "Jesus Christ, Pete! I got you the analysis you wanted. I can't keep doing this—my supervisor was in here yesterday asking questions about who authorized extra time on the mainframe." There was no doubt that he had reason to be nervous—unauthorized investigations were a serious breech of agency rules and regulations. Disciplinary action in such cases began with dismissal and got worse from there. A grave abuse of power could result in criminal charges.

"Yeah," said Pete. "I'm sorry, but I need something else. One more thing and I won't bother you. Promise."

"Nope."

"Mike, come on . . ."

"Hey, look, Pete," said Mike. "It's okay for you—you're the hotshot agent out there in the field. Me, I'm just a desk jockey who has to follow the rules. I want to collect a pension some day. . . ."

Pete was silent for a moment. He truly did not like putting his friend in this position, but sometimes you had to break the rules. "Hey, Mike," he said. "Remember that vacation I'm on. . . . Well, I might not come back from it if I don't get some results. I need your help, man."

Mike Milton squirmed in his seat. "I *hate* it when you do that. Getting all sincere on me like that. . . . Pete, you son of a bitch!"

"Sorry."

"Sorry isn't good enough." Mike sighed heavily. "Okay, what do you want this time?"

"You near your computer?"

"Yeah."

Stupid question, thought Pete. Mike was never far from his computer. "I need to track the action on a secure file. Who's been in, who's been out—all in the last, say, forty-eight hours."

"What?" Mike's voice was full of suspicion.

"The Miami PD file on the break-in at their headquarters the day before yesterday."

"Know the codes?"

"That's what I have you for, Mike."

For the next five minutes, the only sound Pete could hear on the telephone line was the insistent tap as Mike Milton's chubby fingers flew over the keyboard of his computer. Occasionally there was dead silence as Mike hunched over his machine like a grand master over a chess board considering his next move. He mumbled to himself and scolded himself when he made a mistake, but in due course he spoke.

"Okay," he said. "I'm in." Mike sounded slightly out of breath, as if he had climbed a flight of steps.

"Good work."

"Thanks a lot. My ass is really in a sling if someone finds me in this file," said Mike nervously. "In five minutes I am out of here or an internal security trace is going to kick in and lead them straight to my door. Tell me what you need and do it fast, Pete."

"There has got to be something at the Miami PD raid," Pete urged. "Look around . . ."

"Okay." There was more tapping at the keyboard. Then: "Bingo."

"What'd you hook?"

"Miami Police found electronic footprints in their Narcotics Investigation computer from the day of the break-in." Mike worked his keyboard a little more. "That's all there is, Pete. Can I leave now. . . ."

"Hold on—footprints? What do you mean footprints?" He was bouncing all over the room now as Jessie hit the gas and started to burn up the highway.

"It's a series of extraneous commands and codes. Like static on a radio. No one is ever quite sure how it gets in there."

"But what does it mean?"

"Could mean two things—either it was a glitch, which happens all the time or somebody was snooping, which is practically impossible. You can't get any further than I've gone without the passwords and key codes and they probably change every day—maybe even more frequently."

"Earl Leedy could get in," said Pete. Down the line, he could almost hear Mike Milton rolling his eyes the instant he said the name.

"Please Mike—the dead guy?"

"We don't have any proof he's dead," Pete argued

back. "Show me a dead body and I'll believe you. Until then, I'm convinced he's alive and working this scam."

"Well, the Miami police don't agree." Pete could hear Mike moving the cursor as he read off the screen in front of him. "They still think the break-in was a theft that turned violent. They say someone was after the cocaine in the evidence room. Wouldn't be the first time someone ripped off an evidence cage. . . . Remember, in New York? Back in the seventies . . ."

"I remember. That was heroin and it was worth something like ten–twelve million dollars. Nobody breaks into police headquarters and takes that kind of risk for fifty thousand dollars worth of drugs. That was just a diversion."

"For what?"

"For what ever the hell it is that Leedy was up to, that's what."

"Yeah?" said Mike. "Well, I wouldn't broadcast that theory if I were you, Pete."

"It makes more sense my way. All I know is you don't bust a computer genius out of a 747 to steal a little white powder. There's something bigger going down."

"Yeah," said Mike. "And I have a feeling I know what it is, too."

"You do? What?"

"You," he said. "In flames."

16

The next morning around eight A.M., the camper rolled to a halt at the drop zone in northern Virginia and Jessie and her crew—bored, cranky, cramped and bleary-eyed—stumbled out.

"I don't believe it," said Pete, yawning. "I can't believe that we finally got here."

If he could help it, he would not be making that trip again. Jessie, and later, Selkirk, had driven like maniacs all the way up the eastern seaboard. They did not stop to eat, drink or sleep because they reasoned that the ratty old camper had all the comforts of home.

Of course, for Jessie it *was* home. However, she had never noticed that her home lacked adequate suspension, comfortable seats or shock absorbers less than fifteen years old. To Pete the ride had felt like twenty-three hours in a blender.

It didn't take long for all of them to forget their nightmare ride. The drop zone was packed with jumpers from all over the country, the Fourth of July Washington, D.C., jump being the highlight of skydiving season. Swoop, Jessie and Bobbie ran into dozens of old friends in the organizers' tents—Selkirk and Pete felt a little left out—and they saw a number of faces they could have done without: notably Torski and Kara.

At nine sharp the jump master called the meeting to order and climbed up on the makeshift podium to lay down the ground rules.

"The jump tomorrow will be one to tell your grand-children about—"

"Hell, yeah!" someone shouted from the back of the crowd.

"We'll be jumping into the city's fireworks display and coming down in Potomac Park."

Swoop turned to Jessie and gave her the thumbs up. "I love jumping through fire."

"Then you've come to the right place," said Jessie. "There's going to be a lot of fire in the sky."

Pete heard this comment and shook his head. There seemed to be no end to Swoop's capacity for thrill-seeking. Selkirk saw him and smiled. "You know the skydiver's motto: if your life is dull—risk it."

Pete tapped his temple. "Very smart."

The jump master unveiled a huge chart on the stage. A long series of diagrams showing the formations of the next day.

"We are going to build ten five-man stars and send another ten through one star and then through another. Today the judges will make the final choices of who jumps and who stays home. . . .

All over the vast room skydivers looked over their rivals. Pete could tell that they were all thinking the same thing: *you poor bastards . . . came all this way for nothing.* . . .

"If you want to go to the big show in D.C., your team has to score ten formations or better. Alternates must qualify"—Pete could feel his whole team looking sideways at him—"and if there are any questions ask me now or see your team leader." The jump master paused for a moment, waiting to see if there were any questions. There were none.

"Okay. Load up."

They had a whole airport and drop zone to play in—yet Ty Moncrief's team plane was assigned the hard stand right next to Winona's. Torski guffawed when he saw Jessie and her ragtag crew.

"Hey Swoop!" he shouted. "How did a guy like you fix in with a group like that, man? It's embarrassing. If that happened to me—hell, I'd give up jumping. I'd be ashamed to show my face."

Kara laughed. But Swoop said nothing. He just kept his head down and walked to the plane.

Selkirk, however, couldn't help himself. He cupped his hands around his mouth. "Hey! Go fuck yourself!"

"Wasn't talking to you, sonny," said Torski. It looked like the big man was going to be content to leave it at that. But as he walked by Selkirk he grabbed the rip cord for the reverse chute and tugged hard. The small chute exploded from the pack, knocking Selkirk on his butt.

Torski put his hands on his hips and stared at Jessie's crew, daring one of them to take him on. Pete glanced over and decided it was a challenge he would accept. He took a step in Torski's direction, only to feel Jessie's firm hand on his forearm.

"Let it go," she said, her voice low. "Some people always pull this shit before a jump. They think they're psyching you out. It's bullshit. Pay no attention." She slapped him on the back. "Concentrate on the sky."

Pete nodded. "Right."

Torski winked at Swoop. But Swoop did not respond with anything more threatening than his sly, Mona Lisa smile, staring at the sky cowboy. Swoop did not like Torski dumping on his team. . . . Torski did not notice Swoop's fixed smile turning a little bit scary.

To Jessie's surprise, her team pulled off their assigned formations in record time. Pete had been assigned the simplest and lowest profile part of the maneuver and he managed to scrape by without attracting too much attention.

Their points had been allotted before they got to the ground—they scraped into competition by the skin of their teeth, scoring an eleven. Pete knew he hadn't done much to help—if it hadn't been for the superior skills of Swoop and Jessie, they would have finished out of the money.

Ty Moncrief's team jumped alongside Jessie and her divers. Pete realized you didn't have to be an expert to appreciate the skill and finesse of that pack. They racked up eighteen points, the highest of any team in competition.

Swoop was the last of Jessie's crew to head for the ground—Torski the first of his. Swoop had been watching Torski closely, the anger he felt for the Texan feeling like a cold lump in the middle of his chest. The competitive jumping out of the way, Scoop decided it was payback time. . . .

Cutting a downward turn toward Torski, Swoop sailed directly under the man and, without hesitation, pulled his safety knife from his belt and cut away his main chute. The vast canopy floated away, enveloping Torski in an ocean of nylon, like a kid having a bed sheet nightmare. It was a taunting, in-your-face maneuver known as "gift wrapping."

Torski roared and cursed, flailing in the cloth, blinded, unable to see the ground. He had to guess where he was, coming in fast and hot, a hard landing that he couldn't hold, falling and skidding across the drop zone on his ass. He looked very stupid—but worse than that, he looked like an amateur.

The instant Torski stopped skidding he jumped to his feet and went charging across the field, heading for Swoop. Torski could taste blood. But before he could get too close, Kara and Deputy Dog tried to cut him off.

"Torski!" shouted Kara, wrestling him. "Forget it!"

"The hell I will!" the big man roared. "I'm gonna tear that little bastard apart!" He threw aside his two teammates and charged. Swoop stood his ground, smiling his little smile. But just before Torski reached him, Ty Moncrief intercepted.

"Eyes on the prize, Torski," he said calmly. "Eyes on the prize."

Torski stopped and snorted like a bull, doing his best to suppress his anger. He was very red in the face and his fury had built up within him like a hot head of steam—for a second or two it looked like he would burst from the pressure of his rage. Then he took a series of deep, deep breaths, sucking air into his lungs as if oxygen was an anesthetic, forcing himself to calm down. To give vent to his anger, he looked over at Jessie and her team, spat in the dust and then walked away, falling in step with Kara and Moncrief.

"I wonder if they're giving points for the most assholes on one team," said Jessie. "I mean—first Torski and now I see he's jumping with Ty Moncrief. Of course, Kara isn't exactly a lady either. . . ." She squinted against the sun and watched Moncrief's team walk away. She had never encountered Deputy Dog and didn't know a thing about him, but she could guess. "I don't know who the other guy is but I'm prepared to bet he's an asshole too."

Pete was interested. "The guy who stopped Torski," he asked her. "Who's that?"

"Ty Moncrief."

"Know anything about him? What's his story? Where did he come from?"

Jessie shrugged. "Military or something, I think. Good jumper—I'll give him that. But you don't see him all that often. He turns up for the big jumps every now and then. Things like this . . ."

"So how come he's on your shit list?" Pete asked.

"Haven't you noticed, Nessip? Just about *everybody* is on my shit list."

Pete grinned. "Jeez, now that you mention it . . ."

Jessie started back toward the camper, but Pete knew that in spite of her breezy put down, there was a lot more to the story, that there was something between Jessie and Moncrief that she did not want him to know.

It turned out there was one like it just about everywhere. In Ocean Reef it was Alabama Jacks. In Northern Virginia, the watering hole where jumpers congregated was called the Burn In Bar and it was a virtual copy of its cousin to the south, minus the marina and the fishermen—this place was all skydiver. The night before the big D.C. boogie, it was packed to capacity. Divers crowded into the joint, sucking down beers and watching the action of the day being replayed on the video monitors mounted all over the room. They screamed and cheered and pounded the mahogany bar when they saw a maneuver they admired and jeered in derision when somebody messed up.

Torski was there, still nursing a bruised ego, sitting at a table with Kara and Deputy Dog. The three of them were hunched over their mugs of beer, none of them looking up—except Torski who, from time to time, glared over at the table where Jessie's team sat.

It looked as if that was all the big man was going to do by way of reprisal that night—until the tape of his humiliating gift wrapping flashed on the video monitors. From all over the room, people cackled and catcalled.

Torski's grip on his beer mug was so tight it looked as if he would shatter the thick glass in his hand. The muscles in his arm tensed like steel bands and he could feel the veins in his head pulsing.

The tape of the gift wrapping was such a hit that the bartender wound it back and played it again. The bar erupted in laughter once again, then a chant began: *Swoop! Swoop! Swoop! Swoop! . . .*

Swoop sprang to his feet and took a bow. The applause was thunderous. By the time the deafening ovation died away, Torski's chair was vacant. Unable to stand the humiliation he had stalked away into the night.

Swoop was feeling pretty good. It took him fifteen minutes to make his way from his table to the men's room—he was stopped every few feet to get a pat on the back or a kiss from some girl, some of whom would like to have gotten to know him better, but never having jumped with them, conversation was a little difficult. . . .

He had a similar problem in the rest room. Swoop finished up at the urinal, then turned to see that Torski was waiting for him. He did not look happy. The trouble was, Swoop had never jumped with Torski either—so he couldn't even begin to reason with the Texan.

There was no guarantee that any words would have altered Torski's reaction. As Swoop tried to push past him, Torski spun him around and pounded a big, hard fist into Swoop's hard stomach. He doubled over, sucking for the air that had just been knocked out of him. Pure agony raced across his features and he retched from the pain, coughing a little beer onto the dirty floor.

Torski didn't yell or taunt, he just went about the business of hurting Swoop like a journeyman on the job. His left hook rattled the fillings in Swoop's mouth and his right cross slammed him back into a stall. After Swoop slid down the thin partition to the floor, Torski cracked the sharp toe of his cowboy boots into his body. Swoop curled up and tried to protect himself as best he could.

Deputy Dog was standing outside the door of the men's room, warding off interlopers who might interfere with Swoop's punishment. He smiled at Pete when he tried to push his way in.

"Sorry," he said. "Occupied."

"Ooops," said Pete, turning away. "Sorry." Then he turned back and, without warning, landed a sharp elbow in Deputy Dog's ribs. The stab was vicious and painful and it made Dog gasp in pain. He doubled over and sank to the floor, struggling for breath.

Swoop was bleeding from the mouth and nose when Pete burst into the bathroom.

"This ain't about you," Torski growled.

"Fuck with my team, fuck with me," said Pete.

Torski shrugged. "Okay. If that's the way you want to play." He whirled a punch, but Pete ducked quickly and planted a blow of his own. It seemed to travel all the way from the floor and smacked into Torski's mouth, rattling his molars and slamming him back into a line of sinks.

He was hurt, but he wasn't down for the count. And what's more, the big Texan was angry. He came at Pete with everything he had, his big fists lashing out, ready to take Pete down with a single powerful blow.

Had he landed a punch he probably would have knocked Pete out, but Torski was putting too much behind his fists—he was off balance and too angry to think clearly. Pete easily stepped inside his guard and rocked him twice with two sharp blows to the face, Torski's teeth crunching in his cheek like a mouthful of hard candies.

The door of the bathroom flew open and Deuce raced into the room. Pete had a moment or two to deal with him, smacking him around a little, until Bobby came bursting in to take over for him.

Torski gave it one more try, coming at Pete with the last of his strength—but it was too late. The fight was over, but Torski wouldn't lie down—so Pete had to put him down. He drilled him with a quick flurry of blows—chin and stomach—until Torski collapsed in a heap.

Bobby, Selkirk and Jessie were standing in the doorway of the bathroom, looking at Pete as if they were seeing him for the first time. And they liked what they saw.

"Where the hell did you learn to fight like that?" Bobby asked.

Pete rubbed the broken skin that had split across his knuckles. "Cub scouts," he said. "Didn't everybody?"

Swoop was slowly picking himself up from the floor, wiping a gout of blood from his nose. "Jessie," he gasped. "Do me a favor. . . . Tell the new guy thanks for me, would ya . . . ?"

17

In a Winnebago on the far side of the drop zone campsite, Ty Moncrief sat Leedy down in front of a computer, like a parent compelling a recalcitrant child to do his homework. On the VDT screen, the floor plan of a building glowed.

"The Fourth of July comes once a year," said Ty. "That's tomorrow, Leedy. It's now or never and you keep wanting to make it never. . . ."

Leedy nodded weakly, a sick, stricken look on his face.

Torski was slumped in a corner. Kara was standing over him, cleaning the bloody cuts on his face.

"That marshal can still close us down before we jump," Torski grumbled. Even before he got the tar beaten out of him, Torski wanted to kill Pete. Now the desire was so intense he could taste it. "Give me the word," he said, "and I'll take him out now."

Ty Moncrief shook his head. "No. Not yet."

"Why not?"

"If Nessip had anything on us he would have made his move. He wouldn't have let it go this far."

"Then what do we do?"

"I say take care of him—now," said Torski.

"Listen, it's so simple. Cops can smell dead cops from fifteen miles away," Moncrief explained. "All we have to do is keep their team on the ground and they'll never touch us."

Kara was a lot quicker on the uptake than Torski or Deputy Dog. She nodded. "Crossman," she said.

"That's right," said Ty. He leaned back in his chair. "Terrible thing, sky diving. It can be a very dangerous sport. . . ."

A similar scene was unfolding in Jessie's camper. She was busy putting disinfectant on Pete's bleeding knuckles and binding up his wrenched wrist.

"So tell me about this Moncrief guy," he said, wincing as the alcohol flowed into his cuts. "What's his story?"

"The worst," said Jessie curtly. "The guy is the worst news going."

"How come? How do you know him?"

"Jagger did a couple of drug carries with him, three, maybe four years ago. At first, everything was okay. They would meet a plane from Colombia down in the Bahamas—on Green Turtle Cay, I think. . . ."

"Yeah? Then what?"

"Turns out Moncrief isn't a smuggler."

"What is he?"

"Snitch," she said. "Right after Jagger met Moncrief, guess who gets busted and guess who manages to slip through the net?"

Pete considered this for a moment. "Is Moncrief a good enough skydiver to be one of the people I'm looking for? Could he have taken out that 747?"

Jessie laughed and shook her head. "If I find out he killed Jagger it won't matter how good he is." She tied off the bandage on his wrist. "How's that? Too tight?"

"No it's fine. . . ." Pete closed his eyes. " 'Course, if

Moncrief *was* one of the hijackers why would he or any of them take the risk to be walking around here? What's so special about this jump that they'd show up at all?"

"See," said Jessie with a big smile. "You haven't figured us out yet, have you? This is the biggest collection of crazy ass skydivers in the country—anything for kicks. And the Fourth of July means that for one night Washington D.C. is a drop zone."

"So what?" said Pete. "What difference does it make where you touch down?"

"Washington is different. Any other day of the year it's the most restricted air space in the world. *That's* why every skydiver worth his ass wants in on this load. Three hundred and sixty-four days a year they'll shoot your ass out of the sky. Once a year they say 'come on down'— you don't want to miss something like that."

Pete thought about this for a moment. "Where exactly does this jump put down?"

"Wait . . ." She pulled a large scale map of downtown Washington D.C. from one of the duffel bags packed with equipment and spread it on the table. Most of the area in and around the city was bordered in red and marked "restricted" in bold block letters.

"Our nation's capital," said Jessie. "And it's about to be invaded by a bunch of crazy skydivers—and we're being invited. Wild, huh?"

Pete's eyes did not leave the map. "Yeah, really crazy . . . What's the security like?"

"Swoop plans on landing right in Abe Lincoln's lap," said Jessie. "I mean, the cops, the Secret Service— everybody has been alerted to the drop. If a skydiver comes down where he's not supposed to—for once they're not going to shoot on sight. Believe me, it's a nice change."

He ran his fingers across the map. "The White House . . . the Capitol Building, the Treasury, Justice—even over here"—he pointed across the river to suburban Virginia—"the Pentagon. . . . No one is going to believe me, but they could land anywhere in Washington D.C. Anywhere they want and no one would suspect anything, right?"

"Right. You know what people are going to say— those crazy sky junkies, more guts than brains." Jessie shrugged. "Speaking of which . . . I'm headed down to the Burn In—want to come along?"

Pete's mind was elsewhere, still pondering the possibility of some kind of airborne attack on a target in the heart of Washington D.C. He completely missed her gesture, her offer of a friendly drink—a definite breakthrough that passed him by altogether. "Gotta go," he said brusquely.

Tom McCracken was just leaving his office at the Department of Justice, tired after a long day here at head office. The last thing he needed was to be harassed by the beat-up, dirty-faced bum who was loitering around the entrance of the building. McCracken was already fishing for a quarter—easier to pay him off than to get into a big harangue, when the street person spoke his name.

"Hey, Tom . . ."

McCracken peered into Nessip's face. "Pete . . . Oh my God, look at you." He knew that his agent had been traumatized by his brother's death and nearly driven crazy with the guilt . . . but he never expected this. "Holy shit, Pete! What the hell happened to you?"

"Let's go inside and talk about it." Pete nodded toward the building.

"In there? Don't you think you'll look a little . . . out of place?"

"I'm undercover."

McCracken's face darkened. "You better not be . . . ." He thought for a moment. McCracken figured he owed Pete a hearing, even if only on the strength of past performance and loyalty. "Okay. Come on . . . ."

It was well after working hours so the halls of the Justice Department were not crowded. McCracken was pretty sure he had managed to smuggle his unkempt agent into his office without anyone paying too much attention.

"I need to know about an informant. A snitch named Moncrief," said Pete. "He works the drug routes in South Florida."

"Why do you need to know?"

"Because he's part of the case."

"Case? What case?"

"The hijacking case, Tom. I'm right in the middle of it now."

"Don't start with that, Pete. You're in enough trouble as it is. . . ."

"Tom, just pull up Moncrief's profile—please."

McCracken snapped on his computer. "Working undercover while on suspension violates your sworn oath, not to mention about twenty different laws." He typed some commands into his computer. "And me doing this, accessing this file makes it twenty-one."

"I'm in the middle of them, Tom," Pete said urgently. "I've found the chute used on that 747."

With a slow shake of his head, McCracken looked at Pete—there was almost pity in his eyes. "If you've got the evidence, Pete, make your case to the FBI. If you haven't, your career will be terminated in twenty-four hours—and I'm not kidding. Your career will be over and I won't hesitate to sign the papers. Got it.''

''Got it.''

McCracken glanced at the data scrolling on to his screen. ''And you're going to have to do better than Ty Moncrief. That's not going to fly.''

''Why not?''

''Because he's DEA.''

Pete jumped to his feet, stunned by that piece of information. ''Moncrief is DEA?''

''Well, he was. Not anymore. He was honorably discharged just about eleven months ago. . . .''

''Anything else?''

''Just a minute,'' said McCracken. ''His service record is coming up now.''

For a second, text filled the screen then it vanished, the neat columns of text replaced by a jagged slash of gibberish, a field of snowy computer-generated gobble-dygook.

''What the hell is going on here?'' McCracken pounded the keys, trying to subdue the rebellious machine. ''The whole thing is going haywire. Goddamn computers! Pete, I—''

But Pete was gone, racing down the empty corridors of the Justice building. The instant the computer began to crash, a single thought had popped into his head: Leedy.

Jessie was down at the Burn In Bar, her camper was dark—and unlocked. It didn't take a lot of skill or even very much time, for Torski and Deputy Dog to slip inside, find her parachute packed in its green and black pack—and make a few quick deadly alterations. . . .

18

The Fourth of July dawned warm and muggy, the air damp and oppressive—a typical summer morning in Washington. The sun was not very high in the sky when the jump teams assembled on the drop zone, but the day was already hot, the skydivers sweating in their form-fitting jumpsuits. On the tarmac a dozen planes were revving up, feeding smoke and the fumes of burning fuel into the sultry air.

Bobby and Swoop were their usual unflappable selves, but Selkirk was pacing like a caged animal, nervous and jittery, anxious about the coming jump. He almost jumped out of his skin when the jump master's loud-speaker crackled into life.

"This is the twelve minute call for full dress rehearsal," he announced. "Let's get it right, folks, because there's no room for error here. . . . Good luck!"

Jessie looked over her team. "Anyone seen Nessip?"

Bobby and Swoop shook their heads. Selkirk was too preoccupied to answer.

Jessie checked her watch. "Great alternate, huh?" She glanced over at Selkirk. He was so high-strung this morning he seemed to make the air around him vibrate. "What's your problem, ace?"

Selkirk avoided her steady gaze. "Nothing," he muttered, hoping she would let it go.

But she didn't. "Selkirk, what's wrong?"

The mechanic swallowed hard and forced himself to look at her. "You guys are pros," he said with a shrug. "I'm not . . ."

"So?"

"So I don't want to be the one to mess up this jump, that's all."

Torski wandered by, heading for the Moncrief team plane. He grinned at Selkirk—even an oaf like Torski could read the signs of extreme nervousness. "Hey kid," he shouted. "Last practice . . . lotta pressure. Watch them nerves. Don't fuck up." Torski roared with laughter and ambled away.

Selkirk was so scared he couldn't respond. He felt as if his throat was closing, his mouth dry as sand. He was turning into a basket case and Jessie knew it. She slipped her parachute rig off her shoulder and handed it to him.

"Take this," she said.

Selkirk blinked. "*Your* rig, Jess?"

She nodded. "That's right. This rig has logged two world titles. One for Jagger and one for me. I'll jump your rig. Just do it, okay?"

"Are you sure?"

"Of course I'm sure. Take it."

Selkirk took the parachute as if she had offered him the Holy Grail. Quickly, he buckled into it, his chest swelling a little in pride.

Winona was flashing a thumbs-up from the cockpit.

"Okay," said Jessie. "Let's roll."

Winona was as good at her job as Jessie was at hers. She took the plane up to jump height, flying in tight formation with the other aircraft in the flight, travelling steady in wingtip to wingtip perfection. Exact air positioning for a complex jump with other teams was half the battle—if you didn't start out right, the chances of making up lost ground and finishing on target were slim, no matter how experienced the crew.

Up until the moment they reached their altitude, Jessie's team had affected their poses of a studied nonchalance—except for Selkirk, of course—but the instant they found themselves on course their adrenaline levels skyrocketed and they got psyched up, big time.

The four jumpers crowded the door: Bobby first, followed by Selkirk and Swoop—Jessie was last out. Selkirk glanced over at Jessie who shot him a wink—he answered with a fist pump. His nervousness was gone now. He fingered the shoulder straps of his world championship rig and figured that he could do anything. Jessie smiled to herself when she saw it—the kid's enthusiasm was infectious.

Winona leaned back in her seat and gave them the high sign and they dumped, rolling out into the slip stream with an elegant economy of movement, speeding through the open air as precise and controlled as dancers.

Jessie whipped her team through their drill, gathering them up and making them mesh with the other jumpers in their unit. They hooked up with their counterparts and raced through an eight-way block. A double opal—two parallel lines of interlocked divers—followed by the tricky 360 degree inter, a maneuver in which the divers pair off, turn through the entire compass, swing back into a double opal, then without stopping to regroup charge straight into a 180 degree inter. From there they get into star formation and break.

No one put a foot wrong. They carved through the air

flying like they had wings, Selkirk in particular moving with a grace and confidence he had never shown before. He knew he was flying better than he ever had before and by the time the jump master signalled an end to the routine, he was shrieking and hollering in delight, his deliriously happy voice being carried away on the wind.

Ty Moncrief's team had done their part too, but without any of the fire and fervor of the others. They were—literally—going through the motions, performing with a machine-tooled technical quality but without an ounce of joy. They had other things on their mind. Torski, however, was looking forward to the end of the jump. He enjoyed watching people die—particularly if he had a hand in their demise.

Led by Moncrief, the team tracked away from the assembled jumpers first, diving down fast for one of their showy low openings.

Jessie signalled her quad out and they tracked out of formation, their canopies inflating like great splashes of color against the great blue dome of the sky. As she drifted to the ground, Jessie allowed herself a little pat on the back. She hadn't had much time—but she had whipped this ragtag bunch into a team and she was proud of that.

Then: Selkirk's rig began to waffle, like the sails of a ship falling off the wind. He was falling fast, too fast to make a safe landing and he knew it—suddenly his triumphant victory whoops ceased and he looked up, staring at his chute. Jessie could see him clearly, his face ashen as he tugged furiously at his steering lines in a vain attempt to correct the malfunction.

Jessie looked at the altimeter strapped to her wrist. She was at four thousand feet which put him at about three thousand—if he didn't slow down that meant that Selkirk was just fifteen short seconds away from burning in.

Through his fear, Selkirk was having a hard time believing that Jessie's rig could be screwed up. He knew that she was a stickler for safety, inspecting her chute obsessively and packing it with the care of a doctor performing surgery. Even though he was about to die, a single, illogical thought raced through his mind: cut away the main canopy and Jessie'll be *pissed* . . .

Swoop had seen that Selkirk was in trouble and knew exactly what to do—and he had no such reservation about vandalizing the talismanic parachute rig.

"Cut away!" he screamed. "Cut away the main and open your reserve."

But Selkirk looked frozen in his harness, as if he had accepted his fate.

Jessie dropped by him, unable to reach him, but Swoop was still at altitude. He pulled out his own safety knife and slashed through his lines, cutting away his parachute, returning to free fall. Liberated from the huge drag of his canopy, Swoop plummeted, chasing after Selkirk.

The other skydivers in the area were screaming and gesticulating, miming the action of cutting away the chute, begging Selkirk to react. Suddenly, like a man waking up from a deep trance, he began to struggle in his harness. His knife came out of the sheath on his belt and he slashed away at the lines. Before Swoop reached him, Selkirk had cut himself free, pulling his reserve rip cord and waiting for the reassuring tug as the second chute caught the air.

It did not come. The reserve chute did not deploy but remained trapped in the pack on his back.

Two thousand feet . . . eight seconds.

Swoop pushed his head down and streamlined his body into a no lift dive, transforming himself into a human missile, chasing after the panic-stricken Selkirk.

He was half turned in his harness, his arms crossed over his shoulders trying to dig his reserve chute from the pack. He tried not to look down. The ground seemed to be rushing up toward him at a dizzying rate of speed.

Now Swoop was in danger. He had almost reached Selkirk, but if he didn't deploy his own reserve chute in a great big hurry, he was going to hammer in right on top of him.

Jessie scarcely dared to look at her altimeter. One thousand feet . . . four seconds.

Swoop grabbed Selkirk and stuffed his hand into the reserve pack, then yanked his own rip cord, using the shock of that opening to rip out Selkirk's reserve. They were so close to the deck that Selkirk's canopy did not have time to fully inflate and he dropped away from Swoop, a short scream to the ground. He slammed into a marshy canal far to the left of the main drop zone. As Swoop came in on his own reserve, he passed over Selkirk. He was lying very still.

A second later Swoop hit the ground hot, making a hard landing that seemed to dislodge every bone in his body. He scored a couple of bruises on his hands and knees that he knew he would be feeling for a month to come.

People and emergency vehicles were racing across the open ground now, a great circle of onlookers gathering around Selkirk's body. Jessie pushed her way through the crowd, shock and horror on her face. As Swoop dug himself out of the dirt she turned on him, crazed and frantic.

"He was flying my rig!" she screamed. "Why didn't he pull the reserve? Why didn't he pull!"

"He tried," said Swoop. "It didn't open!"

"Bullshit! I packed it myself."

Suddenly she felt the accusing eyes of a hundred spectators boring into her—but she didn't give a damn what they thought. She dropped to her knees next to Selkirk and pressed her ear to his chest. There was a faint heartbeat.

"My God! He's alive!"

"Move it people! Make way!" Two paramedics elbowed their way through the crowd and got to work, feverishly going through the procedures to stabilize Selkirk's shocked and traumatized body. They put an IV in his arm and locked his head and spine in place with inflatable cushions and a brace-belt. Very carefully they moved him onto a stabilizing board and then wheeled the gurney through the crowd to the ambulance that had backed up to the crash site.

Jessie stayed with the rolling cart every step of the way, holding Selkirk's hand until they loaded him into the ambulance. The siren squealed and the vehicle raced away. She felt alone in the crowd and she looked up, hoping that Swoop or Bobby or Pete—someone—was there with her. But the first person in her field of vision was Torski. He was looking at her with obvious surprise, amazed that it was Selkirk, not Jessie, lying broken and bleeding in the back of the ambulance. He looked away quickly, hoping that she hadn't seen him, then tried to lose himself in the dwindling crowd. Torski fell in with Kara and Moncrief, walking away toward their trailer.

Jessie's eyes hardened as she watched, her angry stare following them. "It was them," she whispered. "Just like Jagger."

"What are you talking about?" said Bobby.

"Nothing . . . never mind." She walked away from Bobby and Swoop and made straight for the camper. She found Pete's Beretta in his duffel bag, right where he had left it. . . .

19

By the time Pete returned to the drop zone, the commotion was over and the crowd had dispersed. Some people stood around discussing the near burn in and a few watched the tapes over and over again on the monitors—but Pete paid no attention.

He had other things on his mind—going all the way back to the day of the crash, there had been computer glitches and malfunctions. Those coupled with the computer footprints that Mike Milton had discovered in the Miami PD files—well, as far as Pete was concerned, that all pointed, incontrovertibly, to Earl Leedy.

All he needed was proof—and he found it at the drop zone. Right at his feet. As he crossed the open landing area, making for the campsites he heard something that stopped him dead in his tracks.

"Meow," said Agnes.

He looked down at the fat white cat. It was rubbing up against his shins and mewling for affection or feeding—or both.

"Agnes?"

The cat stared at him for a moment, then decided that Pete did not look like much of a candidate for love or food and then hurried away, running for a hangar nearby. Pete followed. All cats looked more or less the same to him and he couldn't be sure that this creature was Leedy's or not—still the coincidence was too remarkable.

Feeling faintly foolish about trailing a cat, Pete walked along behind, watching as she disappeared through a small hole in the sheet metal walls of the hangar. He dropped to his knees and peered through the rust-edged opening. As he looked, the hangar was filled with the roar of twin airplane engines and the noisy rattle of the hangar doors opening. The plane was moving out onto the runway, ready for takeoff.

Pete recognized it in an instant—it belonged to Ty Moncrief.

"Bingo," he whispered. He took off, running after the plane as fast as he could.

He got to the tarmac, getting there just in time to see the DC3 carrying Ty's team and the rest of his formation lift off the runway.

"Shit!" He ran after it for a few steps, then realized it was futile. The only thing he could do was run toward Winona's plane, the next in line for takeoff. He hauled himself into the aircraft, out of breath.

"Where's Jessie?" Bobby yelled.

"I don't know. She's not here?"

"No one knows where she is." Bobby was beside himself with anxiety and anticipation. "I checked with operations, I checked the hospital—no one has seen her."

"Hospital?" said Pete. "What hospital?"

"You haven't heard?" shouted Bobby. "Selkirk burned in."

"Jesus!" It took a moment for it to dawn on him that he, the alternate, was supposed to take over in the event of a team member dropping out.

"Yeah," Bobby continued. "Right after Selkirk

flamed, she said that Torski and his pals had arranged it—and no one's seen her since.''

Pete rushed up to the cockpit and pounded Winona on the shoulder. ''Get this plane up!'' he yelled. ''I'm going after Ty's team.''

''What the fuck is going on?'' Bobby demanded.

''I'm a US Marshal. You can read about it in the papers later!''

Bobby and Swoop exchanged a look. ''No way later,'' Bobby shouted. ''Winona! Let's go!''

''Right!'' she gunned the engine and the plane picked up speed. She pulled out of their order of takeoff and without waiting for clearance dashed down the runway and lifted off into the sky.

20

Ty's group was seated in the forward part of the old plane, Deuce at the controls. The rest of their formation—eight other jumpers from two other teams—further aft, closer to the jump door. It took fifteen minutes to reach their altitude and a further five passed before they were at their target.

The jump master on board the aircraft gave a hand signal and on his command all the jumpers rose and prepared to dive. The first eight went followed by the jump master, Ty Moncrief's team moving up to the door as space became available. The plane was empty of divers—Ty's group had stopped at the door and went no further, as if they had all had a sudden attack of cold feet.

That was not the case, of course. The team members had stopped to strip off their brightly colored demonstration suits, revealing the jett black covert night suits they wore in a second layer.

Without warning, the door of the baggage compartment flew open and Jessie sprung out, Pete Nessip's nine millimeter thrust out before her. Everyone froze and stared at her. Even Ty Moncrief was surprised to see her, completely failing to foresee a development this unexpected.

"Only one of you have to die," she said angrily. "Which one of you killed Jagger?"

Nobody moved and nobody spoke. Jessie looked from face to face, then her eyes settled on Leedy. He was the weak link—he did not kill Jagger, she was sure of that, but he knew who did and with a little pressure applied he would give him up without a second of hesitation.

Leedy could feel her eyes on him and he started to squirm under her steady gaze, edging away from the rest of his team. Ty was back near the bulkhead separating the passenger compartment from the cockpit. As Jessie held the gun on them, Ty glanced back over his shoulder, making eye contact with Deuce. The pilot knew exactly what was going on. He nodded almost imperceptibly at Moncrief.

"You know," said Ty. "You looked naked without a chute, Jess."

Jessie nodded and smiled grimly. "I figured it was you, Moncrief."

Very slowly, Deuce was sliding his hand toward the throttles controlling both engines.

"What the fuck do you care about Jagger?" said Moncrief. "He let you sit in prison while he came out to play around with Kara here."

Jessie remained cool. As far as she was concerned, anything Jagger may have done in the past was going to stay in the past, where it belonged. The present, however, was a perfect time for some vengeance.

"Nice try, Moncrief," said Jessie, aiming the weapon square in the middle of his forehead. " 'Bye now."

But before she could fire, Deuce jerked on the throttles and pushed forward on the stick. The plane stood on its nose and dove, dropping fifty feet in a few seconds. The floor seemed to vanish under Jessie's feet and her head slammed into the roof of the compartment, the gun flying out of her hands.

Even before the plane was back on an even keel, Torski and Kara pounced on her, holding her down.

"Well, that's a little better," said Moncrief.

Suddenly, a fireworks rocket exploded on the horizon, lighting up the sky and throwing the dome of the Capitol building into stark relief against the night sky.

"It's getting time to jump in and join the party," said Ty. "*Such* a shame that we're going to be blown off course a little bit." He looked over to Torski. "Jessie jumps first."

"But . . . but she doesn't have a parachute," Leedy stammered.

Ty's eyes glittered and he smiled as he looked at her. "Jagger always said she could fly."

Then it dawned on Leedy what Ty planned to do with Jessie. He felt sick to his stomach. Jessie, however, appeared unmoved and unemotional—she looked at the criminal crew with withering contempt.

"Time to go, Jess," said Moncrief. He nodded at Deputy Dog and Kara to grab her, but Jess shook them off and stepped up to the open door on her own.

The fireworks ahead illuminated the canopies of the jumpers who had already deployed, the planes next in line were flying in formation to their jump points. Moncrief's own plane was turning out into open sky. There would be no one to see her fall.

Jessie took one last look at Moncrief and his crew and then, without hesitation, stepped through the opening and vanished into the dark night. Everyone—Moncrief included—was stunned, their mouths dropping open, the display of raw courage they had just witnessed blowing their minds. Except Leedy's. He looked like he was about to blow his lunch.

"Holy shit . . ." said Kara.

"Man," said Ty. "I'll bet she was a great fuck." As far as he was concerned that line would be Jessie's epitaph. He forgot all about her. Then he glanced at his watch. "It's time. Let's go."

Deputy Dog hooked Leedy to a tandem bar and the whole team dumped, falling into the black sky. They tracked away from the fireworks and the other jumpers. Their dark canopies opened as they crossed the river, cruising toward the Pentagon and a group of office buildings set in a carefully landscaped development surrounded by tall trees.

Winona's plane was a mile or two behind Ty Moncrief's. Pete was strapped into his parachute rig and standing behind the pilot's seat, a map of official Washington in his hands.

"I've lost them," said Winona. "But they sure as hell weren't tracking for the fireworks."

Pete stared out the window at the fireworks. "Ty's going home," he said. "He's going to the DEA building."

"What should I do?" Winona asked. "Should I radio for backup?"

Pete shook his head. "No. First they'd laugh at you . . . and then they'd arrest you."

Pete shoved the map under Winona's eyes, showing her the DEA building circled in red. "You've got to get me closer."

Winona looked ahead, scanning the air through her binoculars. "They've got to be out there someplace . . . I don't—Jesus Mary priest!"

"What?"

"Check out Moncrief's plane. The underside."

Pete put the field glasses to his eyes. "Jesus Christ!"

Jessie was holding on to the jumper's foot rail, the length of sturdy metal directly under the jump door. They could see that she was scissor kicking her legs.

"What the hell is she doing?" Bobby yelled.

"I know exactly what she's doing," said Pete. "This is the only trick I know." With that, Pete pulled his goggles down over his eyes and bailed out—as casually as a seasoned jumper, as if he had been jumping out of airplanes his whole life.

Swoop and Bobby looked at each other shaking their heads. Pete appeared to be cut from the same cloth as Jessie—that is, fearless *and* completely crazy.

"No fucking way I'm missing this," said Swoop. "This is going to be fun!"

"Me first," said Bobby.

They both dumped out.

Pete tracked on Ty's plane, coming in fast and just a little below the underside. It was all he could do to control his streaking body—the rest of the rescue was up to Jessie.

She let go of the plane and dropped a hundred feet before she and Pete intersected. He grabbed hold of his rip cord, just as Jessie scissored him with her legs, grabbing hold of him and hanging on with her knees.

Snatching at the rip cord, she pulled hard, the chute deploying instantly and snapping open high above their heads. Jessie held on, wrapping Pete in a bear hug. He worked the controls, trying to keep the chute on track for the DEA building.

Then she realized it was Pete. Her eyes grew wide. "I don't believe it!"

170

"Believe what?" he yelled.

"That it would be you. I thought only Swoop would be able to pull that off!"

"You're welcome," said Pete.

21

Ty Moncrief's team touched down on the DEA roof exactly as planned. And, as in the Miami Police department operation, they worked perfectly, each member of the team performing exactly the function allotted. Kara and Torski went to the roof door, ready to knock out the security, Ty waited with Leedy, Deputy Dog did a quick scan of the roof and peeked over the edge of the building on lookout. Everything was just as Ty said it would be—all except the window cleaning platforms that were tethered over the side, like lifeboats hanging from davits.

Thirty-five floors below in the complex security station in the lobby two guards sat at the alarm control panel, a bank of electronic security grids and video monitors. Seven of the monitors showed gray, washed-out images of ground floor entrances and elevators. The eighth monitor was tuned to a Star Trek episode. One of the guards stared at it slack-jawed.

"Look at this dweeb," said the guard, pointing to an alien. "You'd think that by the twenty-third century aliens would have better looking toupees than that."

The other guard scarcely glanced at the screen. "They all wear wigs on that show."

"Not Spock," said his companion. "He's got them ears."

"What the hell are you talking about?"

On the roof, Torski and Kara slotted electrodes into the magnetic security sensors on the door. Ty plugged the wires into a digital sequencer then launched a program. Numbers rolled rapidly across the screen and only seconds later, locked on a code.

The surge of power through the security system activated one of the sensors on a grid panel in the security room. The two guards looked at each other.

"What was that?"

"A little power hit, maybe?"

"Where's Joanne?"

"She making the rounds. At least, she should be making the rounds. It's her turn."

"Bet she's running the microwave on nineteen." He picked up the phone. "Hey, Joanne, are you cooking again? We've had a couple of power spikes down here."

Joanne was passing through a security checkpoint. She placed her thumb against a glass thumb print reader. The scanner read her fingerprint and the door slid open. She spoke into the microphone clipped to the epaulet of her uniform shirt.

"Cooking? Me? No," she said. "But I'm starved. You guys want to order a pizza?"

Moncrief's team was in the building now, dropping duffel bags down the stairwells and then chasing after them. While Moncrief marched Leedy down the fire stairs to the twentieth floor, Kara, Torski and Deputy Dog stopped in front of an elevator bank on the thirtieth.

Torski pried open the sliding steel doors and forced them apart while Deputy Dog jammed a wedge between them, holding them open. Kara and Torski then tied off ropes, dumped them down the elevator shaft and bailed, skittering down the ropes in a face first rappel, dropping down to a rendezvous with Leedy and Moncrief on the twentieth floor.

Deputy Dog followed them, but stopped a floor above, on twenty-one, disappearing into a crawlspace directly above the ceiling of the twentieth floor. A second or two later, he opened a section of the dropped ceiling and lowered a small mirror on an extension arm through the gap until it came to rest in front of a security camera. The camera was angled to view the corridor leading to their objective, the computer room, but the mirror in front of the camera reflected a portion of the hall, fooling the electronic eye into thinking that it was viewing an empty corridor.

Once the mirror was in place, Torski and Kara darted forward to deal with the fingerprint reader. Kara pulled on a rubber glove while Torski sprinkled the glass front of the device with a fine white powder, gently blowing away the excess, showing a perfect outline of Joanne's thumb print.

Kara placed her gloved hand over the glass, the reader sensing her body heat and scanning the thumb print at the same time. For a very long, unnerving moment nothing happened, then with a buzz and click the door snapped open.

Moncrief and Leedy arrived on the floor just as the door opened. They went through first, while the rest of the team went into phase two of the operation. Torski stood guard on the elevator door while Deputy Dog swung back out into the shaft and started working his way back to the roof.

Leedy had two keyboards this time, both of them patched into the DEA mainframes, and his fingers danced over the buttons, a keyboard for each hand. Leedy was humming to himself, his eyes locked on the VDT screen.

A prompt slotted up: *Restricted Access. Apply Security Code*.

"We're in the game," he whispered. "Now play with me. . . ." Leedy launched a stream of pre-programmed code patterns, numbers flashing across both screens with blinding speed. Suddenly, the torrent of figures came to a sudden and blinding halt, a single number glowing on the screen.

Leedy cackled and rubbed his hands. "How smart can I possibly be?"

Undercover files began popping up, Leedy downloading each as the information appeared on the screen. Kara read over the computer genius's shoulder, amazed that she had found a name she recognized.

"Jimmy Sansome!" she said. "I'll be damned! That asshole used to hit on me when I was in Houston! Never guessed he was a Fed! Jesus, this is going to be fun."

"The keys to the kingdom," said Ty, in awe at what he had put together. There was not a law enforcement undercover, from Maine to Washington, who was safe now—Ty Moncrief knew about every single one of them. He picked up his small radio. Deuce should have landed the plane by now and made it back to the area with the getaway vehicle—Ty's big semi-tractor-trailer truck.

"Deuce, are you ready?"

Deuce was sitting behind the wheel of the truck, parked a few streets away. "I'm here."

Ty glanced at Leedy. "Ready?"

Earl's hands were a blur of motion. "No. There's a lot more information here than I thought there would be."

"Well, we haven't got all night," Ty Moncrief snapped back. His short temper was the only sign of his nervousness.

• • •

Pete and his team crashlanded on the roof of the DEA building, coming in fast and hard. Bobby and Swoop hit powerfully—Swoop slammed into a satellite dish and Bobby's chute snagged on an antenna—but Pete and Jessie got in a downdraft and slammed into the side of the building. Bobby wriggled out of his rig, jumped up on one of the window washing platforms and grabbed an armful of canopy, hauling Pete and Jessie to safety.

They looked around the roof and saw the parachutes and the equipment bags belonging to Moncrief and his crew.

"Guess we've come to the right place," said Pete. He slipped out of his own chute, but kept the reserve—he was beginning to realize that an extra parachute always seemed to come in handy. But not as handy as a gun would be.

He rooted around in one of the sacks and pulled out a gun, a nice slim Walther with a full thirteen-slot clip in the handle. He stuffed it in his belt.

Just then, Deputy Dog came through the roof door and stopped, gawking at the sight he thought he was least likely to see—Pete and his team staring back. It took a second to react, but Deputy Dog dropped back, pulled his gun and fired. The bullet slammed into Bobby's arm, spinning him around before he fell to the floor.

Pete hit Deputy Dog hard, grabbing him around the ankles and pulling him down. Together they smashed through the doorway knocking the door closed. The automatic lock activated instantly, locking the rest of the team out of the DEA building.

As Pete and his adversary crashed down the stairs, Pete dug in his waistband looking for his gun. The instant he pulled it out, though, it was smashed out of his hand by Deputy Dog who immediately scrambled after it. But

Pete was too fast for him, spinning and kicking as the man tried to get to his feet. Dog whipped out a long-bladed hunting knife and lunged. Pete grabbed the brace rod off the door and swung, the makeshift club crunching into Dog's ribs, slamming him to the floor. The second blow, to the back of his head, knocked him out cold. The impact knocked off Deputy Dog's headset and it crackled into life.

"Dog, five minutes to exit," said Torski. "Right on schedule."

"Schedule's gonna change," Pete whispered. He picked up the gun and raced back up the steps to the twenty-eighth floor.

Jessie was frantically looking for a means off the roof. There appeared to be only one way—she jumped into the washing trolley, hit the switch activating the electric motor and slowly began descending, crawling down the side of the building.

A buzzer droned insistently on the security control panel. One of the guards stared at it for a moment.

"What the hell is going on?" He grabbed the phone. "Joanne? I've got a circuit tripping here. It says a washing trolley is moving. Check it out."

Joanne was in the small kitchen on the nineteenth floor, munching on a sandwich. She was much more interested in snacking than what the guard was saying.

"I'll get to it in a minute," she said between bites.

"I'd hurry up if I were you. We might be under attack from Klingons."

"Maybe they've got food." Joanne swallowed and her face brightened. "Maybe they're delivering the pizza."

"Just go see what's up, would ya?"

With a sigh, Joanne put down her sandwich and buckled on her thick weapons belt and trudged down the hall to the elevator. She unlocked the elevator with her pass key, thought for a moment and returned to the kitchen, deciding to take the remaining bit of sandwich with her.

Joanne was surprised when the elevator stopped at the twentieth floor. She reached for her gun and put the mouthpiece of her radio to her lips. The doors swept open and she walked out warily, unsure of who or what she might find in the shadowy corridor beyond.

She found Ty Moncrief. And he had a gun on her. Joanna reached for her own weapon, but Ty stopped her.

"Don't be stupid," he said. "There's really no point in getting killed."

Joanne could see that there was very sound reasoning behind this suggestion. She let her gun fall to the floor.

"Now take your radio, call down to your colleagues and tell them everything is fine," he instructed.

Joanne nodded and unclipped the microphone from her uniform shirt. "Ted," she said. "Nothing going on up here."

The guard's voice crackled back immediately. "Roger that, Joanne. We're still getting the washing trolley signal, though."

"Probably just a short," Joanne replied.

"Roger, out."

Joanne clicked off her radio and looked at Moncrief. "Now what?"

"Thank you, Joanne." He raised his gun and fired. In the split second before the bullet pierced her flesh, Joanne looked stunned and confused, as if she thought that she and Moncrief had a deal, an understanding—that she would do as he asked and in return he would not kill her. She learned too late about how unwise it was to trust Ty Moncrief.

The bullet slammed into the poor woman's forehead, killing her instantly. She fell hard, the items in her belt and even the ID card pinned to her shirt scattering across the floor.

A few floors above them, Pete heard the single shot that had killed Joanne and decided it was time to show his hand. As Torski appeared and helped Moncrief move the dead guard's body away from the elevator, Deputy Dog's corpse came hurtling down the elevator shaft and crashed through the elevator ceiling.

"Sonovabitch!" Torski nearly jumped out of his skin and the color drained from his face as he looked at the dead body of his friend.

"He musta screwed up," said Torski.

"Or is something going wrong?" muttered Moncrief.

Torski snarled and jumped into the elevator. He pushed aside Dog's body, raised his gun and fired into the elevator shaft. Hot rounds howled and buzzed in the narrow space like angry bees and Pete, wedged into the side of the shaft, squeezed himself into a tight corner and hoped for the best.

Moncrief dragged Torski from the elevator. "Easy . . . easy. He's gone, man. Gone. We got work to do."

Torski stopped firing. "Jesus Christ!"

Kara and Leedy came running. "What the hell is all that shooting?" Leedy squeaked.

"Shuttup." Ty grabbed Torski by the shoulders and pushed him toward the steps. "Go up top, to the roof and get the rigs ready. Time to fly." He whipped around. "Kara. Check this floor. Leedy, get ready to go." Ty activated the radio mike clipped to the collar of his jump suit. "Deuce? Let's go. We're on our way."

"Gotcha," said Deuce. He started the engine of the

truck and gunned it, shooting through the darkened streets.

Jessie stopped the trolley on the twentieth floor, peered through the window and saw Kara. She was creeping through a series of offices, a maze of open-topped cubicles, a small automatic weapon, a MAC 10, in her hands. There was a lot of bad blood between the two women—now they were going to fight it out once and for all.

Jessie smashed through the window, her gun in her hand. Kara heard the commotion and dove sideways, scrambling through the labyrinth of cubicles. Jessie fired off balance, the bullets lacerating the padded walls of the offices.

Kara dropped to the floor and saw Jessie's feet beneath the partitions only a few cubicles away. She brought her gun up and laid down a carpet of gunfire. Bullets screamed across the floor, ricocheting off chairs and desks, filling the air with shreds of plastic, wood and metal. Bullets blasted into the panels of the ceiling tripping the smoke detectors, the insistent buzz of the alarms struggling to be heard over the crack of gunfire.

The guards at the security station saw the fire alarms go off. They gaped for a moment, then sprang into action, throwing alarm switches across their control board.

"I'm calling back up and the fire department!"

"Where the hell is Joanne?"

The fire bells were clanging throughout the entire structure now and the building was going into a programmed fire emergency shut down. Elevators closed up and started to descend, fire doors automatically bolted shut. Then the lights went out.

• • •

Jessie jumped onto a desk and returned fire, blasting shot after shot until the firing pin just clicked. She tossed the weapon away and dove for cover. Kara saw her and fired, a line of bullets stitching across the wall just above her head. Jessie hit the floor and rolled, hiding behind a photocopy machine.

Crouched down, she could hear Kara creeping through the office, her jump boots crunching on the pieces of glass and debris strewn across the floor. Suddenly, a flash from a copy machine split the darkness in the room and Kara whipped around—just in time to receive the full weight of a body tackle from Jessie.

Filling both her hands with Kara's hair, Jessie slammed Kara's face into the thick glass of the copy bed of the machine, smashing again and again. As bone met glass, the surface cracked like ice on a frozen lake then gave way completely, Kara's head pushing through, a bloody mess. Jessie didn't know if the woman was dead or alive—and didn't care.

As she slowly backed away from the body, a strong male arm locked around her neck.

"I don't know where in hell you came from Jess," Ty Moncrief whispered. "But right now you're going to help me right on out of here." Sirens could be heard now—it was apparent that his plans would have to change.

Escape was very much on Torski's mind too. He had strapped himself into his rig and threw open the door leading to the roof. The instant he saw Swoop he went for his gun, but he wasn't fast enough. Swoop hit him hard, throwing Torski toward the edge of the building.

Torski struck back, punching Swoop, then pinning him, pushing him over the side. Swoop managed to get one hand free and reached for the nylon safety line that ran from the rooftop to the window-washing rig. He yanked on the rope, looping it around Torski's neck.

"If I go, you go too," Swoop gasped.

"I'll risk it," Torski snarled.

Suddenly, without warning, Bobby pounced on Torski and yanked the ripcord and the reserve chute strapped to Torski's back popped open. The parachute dumped out and filled with wind, jerking Torski up and out into the sky. But Swoop still had the gunman tethered to the safety line and as Torski streaked out into the sky, the noose tightened around his neck. The canopy pulled him one way, the safety line pulled him another and Torski was caught in the middle, the life being rapidly choked out of him.

Swoop held the line taut until he was sure Torski was dead, then he let him go, releasing the dead man out into space.

Swoop and Bobby slapped some skin. "Awesome!" said Bobby.

"Man, I gotta go down!" He looked over the side of the building. The streets around the DEA were beginning to fill with fire engines and police cars. He hooked a safety strap on to his belt and started rappelling down the window trolley's cables.

Earl Leedy had formulated his own escape plan. He packed up his computer gear and put on a DEA jacket he had found and was strolling toward the fire stairs. With a little luck he would just walk out of the building using the confusion as cover. But just as he reached the door, he heard a voice.

"Hello, Earl," said Pete. "Long time no see."

Leedy turned and swallowed hard, all color draining

from his face. He did his best to calm his rampaging nerves.

"Good," said Leedy. "I'm glad you're here. You've got them for hijacking, murder, smuggling, animal abuse. . . ." He held out his bandaged hand. "Look at my finger! Look at my ear! I'll testify against all of them."

"Very public spirited of you," said Pete. He spun Leedy around and grabbed his arm, putting him in a hammer lock.

"Let's go."

"Leedy, just when I thought you had the team spirit." Ty Moncrief stood in the doorway, his arm still locked around Jessie's neck, a gun pressed to her temple.

"I stalled them for you," said Leedy weakly.

"Of course you did . . ." Moncrief looked hard at Pete. "Yes, I see now the resemblance to your brother. Didn't you ever hear that families shouldn't fly together?"

Ty slowly backed away from Pete, but he did not loosen his grasp on Jessie.

"You're not going anywhere," said Pete.

"I think I am. You want this lovely girl to stay alive, don't you?"

Pete pressed his gun into Leedy's temple. "And you need this little prick alive, don't you?"

"Don't talk like that," said Leedy, his face turning red. "You're an officer of the law."

"Shoot both of these fuckers," Jessie ordered.

"Shuttup!" Leedy screeched.

"What's it going to be Nessip, do we start dealing?"

SWAT police were pouring out of the stairwells and a team came bursting into the room.

"Freeze!" ordered one.

It was all the distraction Ty needed. He fired at the two cops hitting both, but when he turned on Pete, Jessie forearmed him and dove away. Pete came flying in to tackle him and locked together they crashed through the window.

They fell a full story before Pete yanked the reserve chute on his back and, as the canopy deployed, the opening shock jerked Ty loose. In a split second he was catapulting toward the ground.

Deuce saw all the cops and firemen and decided that the rescue was off—Moncrief and the rest of them were on their own as far as he was concerned. He gunned the engine of his truck and started hauling ass out of there—when Ty came out of nowhere, smashing into the hood of the vehicle and then falling under the wheels. . . .

Earl Leedy, still wearing his DEA jacket walked out of the building, trying to look like he belonged. He walked nervously past the cops and guards—and no one gave him a second glance. He was free!

Leedy was just about to step off the curb and into blessed anonymity when something made him look up. A figure—Swoop—was rappelling down the side of the building, dropping like a boulder out of the sky. He hit Leedy boots first, knocking him out cold and then slammed into the pavement himself. Swoop noticed two things. One: he had an incredible pain in his leg. And two: he had enjoyed slithering down the side of a tall building so much he desperately wanted to do it again.

Emergency vehicles were everywhere. Bobby was patched up and ready for his trip to the hospital, but the paramedics couldn't get a damn thing out of Swoop. He just wouldn't talk to them. . . .

"Hey, Pete," Swoop shouted. "Do me a favor and tell these guys my leg is broke!"

Pete turned to Jessie. "Swoop spoke to me. . . . So maybe you'll teach me how to jump really. You know, thirty, maybe forty years from now. . . ."

"You already know how to jump," said Jessie. "You jumped, you lived. Good start . . ."

EPILOGUE

The US Marshal's Service awarded the Medal of Valor, its highest award, to Pete and Terry Nessip, a public acknowledgment that they had been right and the Service was wrong. They made the award ceremony as public as possible, hoping to dispel the cloud of suspicion over the brothers. Many more people turned out for this ceremony than had for Terry's funeral. Cammie and Taylor were there, of course, and Pete hoped that they felt better—though he knew there was no medal on earth that could give them back what they had lost.

However, on the day of the ceremony the only thing hovering above Pete were skydivers—Swoop, Selkirk and Bobby came in for a fly-by, like an airborne guard of honor. Swoop still wore his ancient paisley jams, but in honor of the occasion he wore a tie with his T-shirt.

Tom McCracken was there, of course, and he only had one question for Pete.

"When are you coming back?"

"I'm going to catch up on some rest. Do nothing for a while."

"That makes sense."

The truth was, he wasn't sure he was coming back. He had done what he set out to do. With his brother gone, the U.S. Marshal's Service would never be the place it once had been. He would have to think long and hard about it. Besides, there was Jessie to consider. Since that first kiss, things had gotten serious. Pete smiled to himself wondering what Terry would have thought about his new girlfriend—he had always wanted Pete to date exciting girls, but he probably would have thought that this was going a little too far. Pete's challenge now was to see if he could make Jessie a little less . . . wild.

Jessie, however, had other plans. "You know," she said, "we always jump out of airplanes to the ground, right?"

"*You* always do . . . I don't."

"Well, I've been thinking that it might be interesting to jump from the ground into the sky. . . . It's something I've always dreamed of doing."

Peter had undergone too many near misses recently to even consider it. The campaign to keep Jessie firmly on the ground would begin here and now.

"Keep dreaming," he said firmly.

Two days later, Pete and Jessie stood on the runway of the airport, Winona flying the plane straight at them.

"I'm gonna be dead in thirty seconds."

"Just do what I showed you and hang on."

They were both wearing harnesses, rigs even more durable than anything used to hold a parachute in place. Thick nylon lines ran from the harnesses to the underside of the plane, locking them in place. Pete's breathing was shallow and panicky, the idea that this was actually happening had finally sunk in.

"I can't believe I actually listened to you," said Pete. "I must have been crazy. I want out. And I want out *now*."

"Too late. We're hooked up."

The plane was almost on top of them now, the nose up and the undercarriage leaving the tarmac.

"This is insane!"

Pete and Jessie were jerked into the air with the plane, screaming—one in pain, the other in pleasure—vaulting into the clouds. The two of them were bolting straight into the sky, hurtling through space.

Over the roar of the engines and the scream of the rushing wind, Jessie's voice could just be made out. Her shout was joyous, delirious with exhilaration and the feeling of freedom in the open air.

"Welcome to the sky!" Jessie screamed.